# "You and your siblings have been playing tricks on me."

"Tricks, my lord?" Ginnie widened her eyes.

"Burrs in my boots," Justin began. "A bird's nest up the chimney, causing my chamber to fill with smoke. My hot shaving water replaced with cold."

Ginnie's lips began to twitch. What an inventive family she had! "Birds do nest in chimneys," she pointed out.

"However, nettles do not grow between bedsheets," Justin said through gritted teeth. "Nor do the necks and wrists of shirts sew themselves together. Furthermore, this afternoon while I was taking a bath, every towel in the house miraculously vanished. How do you propose to explain *that* away?"

Her immediate concern for his health faded as a vision of him emerging towelless from his bath rose in her mind. Suddenly she was glad of the table between them.

**Regency England: 1811-1820**

*"It was the best of times,*
*it was the worst of times...."*

As George III languished in madness, the pampered and profligate Prince of Wales led the land in revelry and the elegant Beau Brummel set the style. Across the Channel, Napoleon continued to plot against the English until his final exile to St. Helena. Across the Atlantic, America renewed hostilities with an old adversary, declaring war on Britain in 1812. At home, Society glittered, love matches abounded and poets such as Lord Byron flourished. It was a time of heroes and villains, a time of unrelenting charm and gaiety, when entire fortunes were won or lost on a turn of the dice and reputation was all. A dazzling period that left its mark on two continents and whose very name became a byword for elegance and romance.

## Books by Carola Dunn

**HARLEQUIN REGENCY ROMANCE**

# GINNIE COME LATELY

Carola Dunn

TORONTO • NEW YORK • LONDON
AMSTERDAM • PARIS • SYDNEY • HAMBURG
STOCKHOLM • ATHENS • TOKYO • MILAN
MADRID • WARSAW • BUDAPEST • AUCKLAND

Published October 1993

ISBN 0-373-31208-3

GINNIE COME LATELY

Printed in U.S.A.

# CHAPTER ONE

WHY THE DEVIL had Sir Thomas looked at him so oddly? As Justin crossed St. James's Park from Whitehall towards Mayfair, he pondered the curious reaction of the man to whom he had just tendered his resignation.

His reasons for quitting the diplomatic service were by no means out of the ordinary. His widowed father, Lord Wooburn, was alone at Wooburn Court. As the earl's heir and sole offspring, Justin felt his place was at home now that Boney was beaten. He had stated as much in the sober, discreet, unemotional manner expected of an English gentleman, and more particularly of a diplomat.

No hint had passed his lips of his fear that his aging, reclusive father must be desperately lonely. So why had Sir Thomas appeared first surprised, and then thoroughly embarrassed?

Crossing the Mall, Justin dismissed the question from his mind. He was back in England at last after two years' absence; it was time to marry and settle down to learn to manage the estates that would one day be his. The important question now was whether Lady Amabel had waited for him.

Lady Amabel of the raven locks, Toast of the Town, cool, elegant, sophisticated daughter of the Earl of

Trenton—he scarcely dared hope to find her still unwed. Though he could not but be aware that he was a highly eligible *parti,* he had not wanted to tie her down while he was abroad. Any understanding between them had been unspoken, far too informal to allow such a breach of propriety as an exchange of letters.

Now he wondered whether he would find Lady Amabel in London. The Season was coming to an end. The trees in Green Park were taking on the darker hues of summer. On sunny days like this, the noonday streets were hot, dusty, noisome, and a pall of smoke from sea-coal cooking fires settled over the city.

Many members of the ton had already departed to their estates, but Lord Trenton was very much involved with the government, and his daughter was no lover of the countryside. Nonetheless, she might well be attending a house party anywhere in England.

In that case, should he follow her, or go straight to his father in Buckinghamshire? Of course, if she were married, or betrothed, he'd not have to make that decision.

He reached Curzon Street. The knocker had not been taken down. He made use of it.

As the porter admitted him, the butler approached across the pink-and-white marble floor. "My lord! If I may say so, it's a pleasure to see you back in England."

"Thank you, Roberts." A good memory for names had been an advantage in the diplomatic service. "Is Lady Amabel at home?"

"I believe her ladyship is about to drive in Hyde Park, my lord."

"Lord Amis, is that really you?" The high, clear voice made him swing round. Lady Amabel was descending the stairs, carrying a driving whip. She was a perfect vision in pale rose, frilled and beflounced, with a crimson spencer. The high crowned bonnet set upon her dusky ringlets boasted three curling ostrich plumes, crimson and white. "My dear Amis, I shall take you up with me instead of my groom. I am driving my high-perch phaeton, but I daresay that will not alarm you."

"Not in the slightest, Lady Amabel. I know you for a prime whip." His cool composure matching hers, he bowed over the gloved hand she held out to him. "I should have liked to see you handling the ribbons of a troika."

She tapped his shoulder with her whip. "Ah yes, you have been in Russia, have you not?"

"And Vienna, for several months."

"And are you about to leave again for some distant post?"

"No. I was offered a position in our embassy in Paris, a much-coveted assignment, but I have resigned. I have done my small part in defeating Bonaparte by keeping our Russian allies happy."

"Yes, of course. Waterloo was a splendid victory, was it not? So you are come home for good." Her flattering air of satisfaction vanished as her rosy lips tightened with annoyance. "Roberts, why is my carriage not at the door? I ordered it half an hour since."

"It is just pulling up, my lady," said the butler quickly.

Justin gave her his arm and they went out. The phaeton was a dashing, fragile vehicle with huge wheels, the body, slung between springs, five feet above the ground. Despite his bold words, Justin was relieved to see that at least Lady Amabel drove a pair, not a team of four horses.

He handed her up, admiring her graceful movements in such a perilous ascent, and followed her. Behind the high-stepping but sluggish greys, they set off for the nearby park.

"Tell me about your travels, Lord Amis," she requested, turning south towards Rotten Row.

Knowing she would have no interest in the wretched condition of the Russian peasants, Justin concentrated on the splendours of St. Petersburg and the gaiety of Vienna. As they tooled along, he described the superb Winter Palace, the tsar's fêtes at the Summer Palace, and the magnificent balls that had at times seemed the chief purpose of the Congress of Vienna.

"I should have liked to be in Vienna, and Russia might be quite amusing, for a short while," she said carelessly. "La, how boring it is here, I vow, with everyone going into the country."

"I was fortunate to find you in Town."

"We are off tomorrow to Kent for a week—the Seagrams, sadly dull but Lady Seagram is an intimate friend of my mama's. Then I shall go on to the Parringales, in Somerset. You are acquainted with the Parringales, are you not? Such amusing people. I am sure you can obtain an invitation."

Encouraging words! In fact, she had undoubtedly rejected other suitors to await his return from Russia, he realized. "I must speak to your father before I leave Town," he said.

She gave him an approving glance before returning her attention to her horses. "I am sure Papa will be glad to receive you this evening. We dine at home. If you are not otherwise engaged, perhaps you will join us?"

"With pleasure. However, I shall not be able to join you at the Parringales', I fear. I must go down to Wooburn."

"Of course. How could I forget? A simply shocking situation. I feel for you, Amis, indeed I do, but I dare say you will know how to deal with it."

Justin frowned. "Deal with what? What shocking situation?"

"My dear, never say you do not know! Lord Wooburn has remarried."

"My father married?" Stunned, he stared at her, quite unable to appreciate her delicate profile.

"To a woman he met at Bath, or was it Cheltenham? He was taking the waters somewhere. A common, vulgar female, Pamela Parringale told me, half the earl's age and deeply in debt. They say she claims to be a widow, no doubt to account for her offspring."

"Offspring?" He groaned.

"A dozen or so, *on dit*. La, one cannot blame the creature for wishing to provide for them. Doubtless your papa will come down handsomely, at least while he is in the first throes of infatuation."

"Not if I have anything to say in the matter!" Justin said grimly. How could his father have betrayed the memory of his beloved wife? But no, he was not to blame. The jade had entrapped him. Given half a chance, she would make him miserable and feather her

children's nest at his expense. Well, she'd not have that
chance, he vowed. "Forgive me, Lady Amabel, if I cut
short this delightful outing. Will you be so good as to
return to Curzon Street now? I must leave for Wooburn at once."


"JACK HAS GOT his trousers very dirty," observed
Priscilla with a seven-year-old's inimitable self-
righteousness. "Jimmy is even dirtier. I am perfectly
clean." She smoothed her faded blue muslin skirts and
adjusted her blue-ribboned chip-straw hat.

"Which is scarcely to your credit, since you hate to
be dirty," Ginnie pointed out. The twins were indeed
both muddy and wet, but it was only to be expected
when the frogs were croaking enticingly among the
reeds of the ornamental lake.

"I'm dirty, too," said Nathaniel proudly, holding
out his arm to show his sisters a smudge on his sleeve.
Anything the twins did was perfect in his eyes. At nine,
they were his heroes, his older brothers being too distant in age to be imitated.

Ginnie held his hand tightly. He was too little to join
Jack and Jimmy at the water's edge. When they
reached the beech wood sheltering the east end of the
lake, she'd let him climb on a fallen tree trunk.

This was her favourite walk in her stepfather's park.
The water reflected the deep, cloudless blue of the late-
afternoon summer sky. Yellow flags grew among the
bulrushes, and here and there patches of forget-me-
nots bloomed on the bank. She had seen herons here,
standing hunched unnaturally still in the shallows or
wading with the gravity of aged lawyers. Once, passing one of the occasional willow trees, she had caught

the azure flash of a kingfisher as the shy bird darted
into the shelter of the long, narrow leaves.

No chance of that now, with the twins creating riot
and rumpus, she thought, laughing as she turned to
glance back at them.

"Ginnie, look at my frog!" Jack dashed up to her.
She could always tell them apart, though she wasn't
sure how. Perhaps by the pattern of freckles across
their noses and cheeks.

The little greenish brown creature sat in his cupped
hands, its throat pulsating, seemingly unafraid. Priscilla backed away, making ughish noises. Ginnie
touched it gently.

"You were clever to catch it, Jack, but you must put
it back. It will not be happy away from the water."

"I'll give it to Judith. She'll like it, not like silly
Pris."

"Me, too." Jimmy, mud to the knees and wet to the
elbows, arrived with another captive. Then his gaze
travelled beyond the group. "Look! Who's that?"

Turning round, Ginnie saw a horse and rider emerge
at a gallop from the shade of the woods. Hooves
drummed as they moved from soft leaf-mould onto
the close-cropped turf, speeding nearer. The rider saw
them and abruptly drew rein. The horse, a magnificent bay stallion, reared. The gentleman slid ungrace-
fully over its croup and landed flat on his back, his tall
hat flying from his head.

Ginnie started towards him. The chalky ground was
hard after a dry week and she feared he might be injured. However, he sprang to his feet unaided, so she
turned to comfort Nathaniel and Priscilla, who clung
to her in fright.

Their frogs escaped and forgotten, Jack and Jimmy clung to each other, rocking in fits of laughter. "What a clunch!" Jimmy snorted.

"Hush!" she admonished them. "You will embarrass the poor gentleman. You know you must not laugh at the misfortunes of others."

"Gammon!" said Jack vulgarly. "That wasn't misfortune, he muffed it."

"Pray mind your tongue, Jack. See, he is coming."

The gentleman approached, his beaver and whip in one hand, the stallion's reins in the other. He was a little above middle height, slim, but with the appearance of lithe strength. Though top-boots and buckskin riding breeches were powdered with road dust, his brown coat fitted like a glove and his neat neckcloth had not suffered in the fall.

Nor, it seemed, had he, except in his dignity. His light brown hair was ruffled, and so was his temper. In fact, his expression was thunderous.

His face was vaguely familiar to Ginnie. Without the scowl he must be quite handsome, she guessed.

He looked her up and down in a shockingly insolent manner, from the shabby chip-straw bonnet hiding her golden ringlets to the half-boots of worn jean. Sneering, he said, "So you are the gull-catcher. Mutton dressed as lamb! You need not expect to profit by your chicanery, strumpet. By all the devils in hell, I'll see you damned first!"

Before she could catch her breath, reft from her by the startling attack, he vaulted into the saddle and galloped up the hill towards the house.

Nathaniel burst into tears, understanding the stranger's tone if not his words. Priscilla's lips trembled, and the twins stared after the man, their identical faces aghast.

Struggling to contain her anger, Ginnie crouched to hug her littlest brother. "It's all right, darling. Sticks and stones may break my bones, but words will never hurt me."

"Why did he call you a trumpet?" asked Jimmy.

"Strumpet!" she corrected, outrage sweeping away discretion. "A strumpet is a wicked woman."

"You're not wicked." Tears overflowed Priscilla's eyes.

"What's chickery?" Jack wanted to know.

"Chicory's that blue flower, sapskull," his brother advised him and added, puzzled, "That man must think Ginnie grows it to sell. Why is it wicked to profit from selling chicory?"

"He said 'chicanery.' Trickery. Oh, how dare he!"

"What about gull-catcher?" Jimmy enquired, cautious now. "Judith had that pet seagull once, the one with the broken leg, 'member? But you never caught one, did you, Ginnie?"

"Never," she said grimly. The identity of the churlish gentleman began to dawn on her. "A gull-catcher is someone who lays snares for innocent fools and robs them."

"You're not a robber," wailed Priscilla.

Jack glowered fiercely. "You're not wicked and you're not a robber. Why did that dolt call you names?"

"He said bad words, too," Jimmy pointed out, his sandy brows drawn together.

"You're not even dressed like a lamb," Priscilla said through her tears. "Lambs wear white wool and you're wearing lilac muslin."

Mutton dressed as lamb! Somehow that affront hurt the worst. She was only twenty, after all.

"I like lambs," Nathaniel assured Ginnie, his arms round her neck. He pressed a damp kiss on her cheek.

She returned the kiss, loosened his arms, and stood up. "I have a feeling the gentleman must be the viscount, Lord Amis, our stepfather's heir," she said thoughtfully. "And I believe the odious brute mistook me for someone else. Come, let us go back to the house. I must talk to Gilbert and Lydia."

Gilbert, at sixteen, had a good head on his shoulders despite his choosing to bury it in Greek and Latin tomes. Lydia, a year older and the Beauty of the family, had inherited from their mother a placidity that her more-volatile elder sister always found soothing. Ginnie meant to tell them everything.

Not for the world would she let her younger brothers and sisters know that she had been mistaken for Mama. The new Lady Wooburn deserved such insults no more than her eldest daughter. Less, in fact, Ginnie acknowledged to herself with a twinge of guilt. On her own, Mama would never have made a push to attach the earl. Her eldest daughter had managed the entire business for her.

And a well-managed business it was! That boorish Lord Amis had no notion of the situation and no right to abuse anyone concerned.

Nathaniel's short legs scuttled to keep up with his sister's angry stride as she stalked up the hill to the splendid early Georgian red-brick mansion that was now their home.

"TAKE GOOD CARE of him."

Justin tossed Prince Rurik's reins at the groom, with an abrupt nod in acknowledgement of the man's stammered, "Welcome home, my lord." He strode into the house.

What a ridiculous figure he had cut! Prince Rurik had never thrown him before, but then he had never required the noble, well-mannered beast to stop on a sixpence. Blinded by the bright sun as he left the woods, he had not seen the little group on the bank of the lake until he was too close for comfort.

That the hussy was a most attractive female only made his humiliation sting the worse. A pretty piece despite her simple gown, fit to twist an old man round her little finger. Those filthy brats with her were no more than ten years old, so she was probably under thirty, less than half his father's age. She looked younger, doubtless a credit to the cosmetic arts of the Cyprian.

A fitting subject for the London scandalmongers! The thought of his loved and respected father held up to ridicule made him shudder.

Reaching the front hall, he dropped hat, gloves, and whip on the table, noting the vase of gladioli, scarlet, white, and yellow. Impatiently he brushed at the dust on his coat and breeches as he glanced around. The place breathed an indefinable air of comfort, a far cry from the gloomy atmosphere that had reigned since his mother's death and his father's withdrawal from the world.

Nonsense! Sheer imagination, the influence of the sun shining in through the clerestory below the dome, throwing patches of light on the portraits of his ancestors.

"Reynolds!" he shouted.

Before the echoes of his voice died away, the stout butler puffed into view from the servants' wing. "Welcome home, my lord," he cried, beaming.

Reynolds had ruled the household as long as Justin could remember, and besides, he already regretted having treated the groom so curtly. "Thank you," he said. "It's good to be home. Is my father in the library?"

"No, my lord. His lordship has taken her ladyship out in the carriage, to call upon the Frobishers and the Rills, I believe. That is why no footman was here to greet you. His lordship will be disappointed... is something wrong, my lord?"

Justin realized he was gaping. Her ladyship gone out? Then who the devil was the female he had nearly ridden down in the park, had bitterly castigated as a gull-catcher and a strumpet? A governess, possibly, but he had a mortifying suspicion he had mistaken his stepsister for her mother. That would explain her appearance of excessive youth. He groaned.

"Are you unwell, my lord?" Reynolds asked anxiously. "Your chamber is prepared, has been ready since his lordship received your letter from—"

"I am perfectly well," Justin snapped. "I rode from London, so my valet will not be here for some hours. Kindly send up hot water and someone to pull off my boots."

Taking the stairs two at a time, he made for the apartments that had been his since he left the nursery. Everything was familiar, yet somehow strange, giving an impression of brightness, newness.

That was it: newness. The new countess had already begun her extravagances. He strode to the window of his dressing-room. Yes, these curtains were similar in colour—ochre with a design in dark green—to those that had always hung here, but they were new. The ragged corner, chewed by his setter puppy and badly mended, was now whole.

Why the jade had troubled to refurbish *his* rooms puzzled him for a moment, until he saw the flowers on his dressing-table. Of course, she hoped to win him over. She'd soon learn how vain was that hope.

He took the yellow roses and tossed them dripping out of the window.

As he sucked on a thorn-stabbed finger, his fury burned higher. After two years abroad, to come home to this catastrophe! At least he might have expected his father to be at home to welcome him; but no, he had taken his bride to call upon the Rills and the Frobishers. Years had passed since he had visited or entertained the neighbours. Not only were Lady Wooburn and her family living in clover at the earl's expense, she was a gadabout who was cutting up the old man's peace.

Justin reaffirmed his resolve to spike her guns. He'd begin his campaign this very evening.

# CHAPTER TWO

RECALLING THE TWINS' condition just in time, Ginnie turned away from the porticoed front door and took the children round to the stable entrance. There they found Colin and Judith, admiring the viscount's bay stallion. Leaving them in charge of the younger ones, Ginnie went into the house in search of Gilbert and Lydia.

As expected, she found them in the library, Gilbert with his nose in a book, Lydia keeping him company as she hemmed a shirt. Ginnie paused in the doorway, studying the two heads bowed over the table by the window.

Gilbert was dark, like their father, but serious minded as that light-hearted, ever-optimistic gentleman had never been. He ought to go to university and take orders, or perhaps be called to the bar. With his passion for detail and logic, he'd make a good lawyer.

Lydia was equally serious, but not at all intellectual. In fact, Papa had been wont to call her his pretty ninnyhammer. Now, four years after his death of a fever, pretty was too weak a word. She was beautiful. Her ringlets, of a richer gold than Ginnie's, never needed to be curled in rags overnight. Her straight little nose and rosebud mouth had drawn raptures from the Cheltenham swains, whereas Ginnie's nose was described by one enamoured gentleman as pert, her mouth as generous. Lydia's lustrous eyes, now fixed on her sewing, were speedwell blue, Ginnie's of a blue that just escaped being grey.

Ginnie could not resent her sister's loveliness. Lydia was *good*. She deserved a London Season, not to spend every waking moment setting her tiny, neat stitches, always patient, never complaining.

Ginnie's sigh brought both heads round.

"What's wrong?" demanded Gilbert.

She crossed the room, conscious of the weight of learning, of knowledge and experience, ranged on the ceiling-high shelves about her; it ought to make her problems seem petty, but never did. Pulling out a spindle-back chair, she sat down at the table and leaned both elbows on the polished oak.

"Lord Amis," she said shortly.

Lydia looked blank.

"Our stepbrother," Gilbert explained to her. "He is expected home from Russia, remember?"

"He is come home," Ginnie informed them, "and I for one shall not call him brother! He is the greatest wretch in Christendom, a rude, bad-tempered boor."

"Oh, Ginnie, no," Lydia protested, unwilling to think so ill of anyone.

"What has he done?" asked Gilbert.

She told them, her wrath reviving as she repeated Lord Amis's brutal epithets.

"'Mutton dressed as lamb?'" said Lydia wonderingly. She patted Ginnie's hand. "The poor man must be half-blind."

"Quite possible, at least momentarily," Gilbert agreed, "since he had just ridden out of the woods into the sun. As for the rest, well, you must not take it personally, Ginnie. He doesn't know you, so his words were not really addressed to you, but rather to a concept in his mind."

"But to speak so to *anyone* reveals him as a shocking rudesby. Indeed, it is still more unmannerly to insult a perfect stranger, without provocation, I vow! I wonder that our kind, courteous step-papa has so ill-bred a son, indeed I do."

"He had just fallen from his horse," Lydia said pleading his case. "You know how cross one feels after making a cake of oneself. Besides, even if he did not injure himself, he must have been bruised and shaken, which is enough to make the most amiable person pettish."

"Pettish! Lyddie, dear, you are too tender-hearted to be true."

"It seems to me . . ." Gilbert began, frowning, but the library door slammed open and Colin burst into the room, followed by Judith, Jack and Jimmy, and Priscilla.

"Wait for me!" wailed Nathaniel, trotting in last.

"Don't touch anything, twins," Ginnie ordered her grubby brothers.

"Ginnie, is it true?" Colin demanded, towering over her as he planted both fists on the table, his sun-browned face flushed. "The twins say Lord Amis attacked you. By George, I'll take a horsewhip to him!"

At fifteen, he was tall and sturdy enough to make a good try at chastising the viscount. Ginnie blenched.

"Don't fly into the boughs," she said hastily. "He did ride up to us in a rather alarming way, but he attacked me only with words."

"That's bad enough. I'd call him out but I dare say he'd tell me I'm too young and refuse to fight."

"I should hope so! He cannot possibly be the villain he sounded."

"He sounds perfectly horrid." Judith hugged Ginnie. She had an instinctive sympathy for hurt creatures and apparently counted her eldest sister in that class at present. "Don't let him upset you, darling Ginnie."

"We'll get back at him somehow," Colin vowed. "We can't let him get away with it."

The twins exchanged a glance. "We'll put frogs in his bed," Jack suggested.

"No, you will not!" Judith rounded on them. "Think of the poor frogs!"

"Burrs in his boots," Jimmy said with relish.

"I'll bite him," Nathaniel volunteered from his perch on Lydia's lap.

"Oh no, Nathaniel," Lydia said gently, "you know better than that. Only babies bite people."

"Heavens, what a bloodthirsty family I have," said Ginnie, laughing. "Thank you, my dears, but I don't want any of you to avenge me. After all, he did me no real harm. It was all a misunderstanding. Look at that clock, it's time for your supper. Judith, Colin, take the others upstairs if you please and see that they wash their hands. And the twins had best put on their nightshirts right away."

"All right." Colin plucked Nathaniel from Lydia's knee and set him on his shoulders. "We won't do anything for the present, but Lord Amis had best change his tune or he'll get what's coming to him. Duck when we reach the door, Nat. Come on, fellows." He strode out, whistling "A-hunting we will go," and Judith herded Priscilla and the twins after him.

Ginnie turned to Gilbert. "You are right, I ought not to take Lord Amis's insults personally. He was addressing a—a . . . what did you call it?"

"A concept. A sort of Platonic archetype, an abstract idea that—"

"Pray don't explain! Anyway, he clearly mistook me for Mama."

"For Mama?" Lydia's vivid blue eyes widened with astonishment.

Gilbert frowned again. "That is what I was going to say when the troops arrived. I cannot like it. You are not easily overset, Ginnie, but Mama . . ."

"Mama is not to be told. Lord Amis will undoubtedly come to his senses before he sets eyes on her, and if not, he will change his tune the moment he meets her. Can you imagine anyone suspecting Mama of being a strumpet?"

"She does not match my concept of a strumpet," Gilbert agreed, grinning.

"Gil, you are by far too young to have any concept whatsoever of such a thing! And Lydia ought not even to know the word."

"Nor ought you," he retaliated.

"I am not precisely sure of the meaning," Lydia admitted without great interest.

"Just as well," Gilbert said. "Now do go away, Ginnie, there's a dear. I want to finish this chapter before I have to change for dinner."

Lydia picked up her sewing. "Do you suppose Lord Amis will join us for dinner?" she asked her sister.

"Certainly. He has not seen his father for two years. I believe I shall see what a conciliating gesture can do. Reynolds will know what wine ought to be served, and Cook must know what Lord Amis's favourite dishes are—she has been here forever. I'll ask her if any can be prepared at the last minute, for tonight, to welcome home the heir."

Swinging her hat by its faded ribbons, she went off to the kitchens.

JUSTIN WAS DETERMINED to attain his usual impeccable elegance for dinner. His father would not notice if he went down in his riding coat and breeches, but that dowdy young woman might know more of fashion than her straight-skirted, flounceless gown suggested. He'd not give her more cause to sneer at him.

The evening clothes left in his wardrobe were subtly out-dated; those he had brought in his saddle-bag were inevitably creased. His valet, being driven down from London by his groom, would not arrive for some hours yet. Making himself presentable was going to be a lengthy business, so he rang the bell at once.

His father's elderly man, who came in answer to his summons, pottered off with the creased garments for ironing and sent up a tan-liveried footman with hot water.

When at last the aged valet reappeared, he announced, "His lordship has sent a message, my lord, that he and her ladyship will be dining with the Rills. There will be just your lordship, Miss Webster, Miss Lydia, and Mr. Gilbert at dinner, the other young people taking their supper in the day nursery."

Webster... Justin realized he had not even known the intruders' name. He was tempted to ask about them, but he would not demean himself by gossiping with a servant. No doubt he'd find out all their flaws soon enough, those not already all too obvious.

So his father had even been persuaded into dining out, instead of in the comfort of his own home. But perhaps he no longer found his own home comfortable, with swarms of young Websters about. Justin wondered if he had been precipitate in resigning from the diplomatic service. He might yet come to yearn for it as a refuge.

At last he was ready. He regarded himself in the glass. His pumps gleamed, polished by Tebbutt before he'd packed them. His black pantaloons fitted snugly, as did the coat of the midnight blue he preferred for evening wear. His waistcoat was of the palest blue. He had tied his starched neckcloth, white as the foam of a waterfall, in the complicated *en cascade*, and it had come out perfectly. His hair was brushed forward in the fashionable Windswept style.

Satisfied with his appearance, he frowned, suddenly struck by the dreadful possibility that Miss Webster might take his care in dressing as a compliment. If so, she'd soon deduce her mistake from his manner, he vowed.

He went down to the drawing-room, paused in the doorway, and gave a swift glance round the room. No one was there but the young woman he now assumed to be Miss Webster, a slender figure in high-waisted lavender blue muslin, unmodishly straight and unadorned. She stood by the open French windows, one hand on the doorpost, gazing out at the terrace, the evening-lit gardens, the park beyond. The westering sun turned her ringlets to pure gold, but Justin was more interested in what was going on inside that admittedly pretty head. How she must be gloating over having acquired so magnificent a home!

What he had to say was for her ears alone. He stepped forward and closed the door firmly behind him. She swung round at the sound.

"Miss Webster, I believe?"

"Yes, I am Virginia Webster, my lord." Her voice was wary. With the sun behind her, he could not make out her expression.

He strode forward and took a stand at the other side of the French windows, forcing her to turn towards him. Her blue-grey eyes questioned him, her mouth seemed on the verge of a smile. She was uncertain, but by no means apprehensive, as he would have wished.

With deliberate arrogance he scanned her from head to toe. His rude gaze brought a decided sparkle to her eyes, and the hint of a smile vanished. Her determined chin tilted at a defiant angle. Not a beauty, yet damnably attractive—and far too youthful to be the mother of those children. He could not believe he had made so henwitted a blunder.

"I must make my apologies," he said stiffly. "I was under the impression that you were...Lady Wooburn. However, I accurately expressed my sentiments and intentions towards your mother. The woman who ensnared my father is beneath contempt and I shall do my utmost to see that she regrets her iniquity. My mistake changes nothing.''

"Indeed it changes nothing!" she flared, fists clenched. "Your mistake is utterly insignificant, since it was not Mama but I who promoted the match, by every means in my power."

Eyes flashing with fury, bosom heaving, she was *devilish* attractive. He took her by the upper arms in an ungentle grip and planted a kiss on her soft mouth.

Turning away her head, she struggled to free herself. Her silky hair had a faint fragrance of jasmine. He slipped an arm around her and pressed her against him, while the other hand on the back of her head forced her to raise her face to him. Her heart beat wildly against his chest.

She ceased to struggle. Her eyes were expectant now, almost...taunting? He'd show her he was no gauche gapeseed! Once again he lowered his mouth to hers, explored her tender lips with his tongue, tasting, searching, probing for an opening to the sweetness within.

The click of the drawing-room door latch sounded loud to his heightened senses.

Instantly he released her and stepped back. Shaken, he reproached himself for his ungentlemanly conduct, forcing his attentions on an unwilling female. Turning to the French windows to hide his agitation, he felt her considering gaze upon him before footsteps and the rustle of her skirt told him she had moved away.

"You are very smart tonight, Lydia," she said lightly, her voice untouched by emotion.

Justin's self-disgust changed to anger. Gull-catcher was too mild a word for Miss Virginia Webster! She was a witch. Somehow she had laid an enchantment on him, led him on to abandon propriety and common sense. She was as bad as her mother, or worse. No wonder his unworldly father had fallen prey to their wiles!

He bit his lip as the full consequences of that embrace dawned upon him. She had only to tell her stepfather of his son's shocking behaviour and it would be he who was disgraced.

"Lord Amis, may I present my sister Lydia? And this is Gilbert, my eldest brother." Ginnie was proud of her even tone. She hoped she did not look half as pink cheeked and dishevelled as she felt. If Gilbert guessed the familiarities she had been subjected to, he'd soon forget his philosophical attitude.

She would never be able to persuade him that she had rather enjoyed Lord Amis's embrace, once she had resigned herself to it. She had been kissed before, but never so expertly, and she suspected she had only experienced the half of it. She had felt positively weak at the knees! If Lydia and Gilbert had not come in... On the whole, she felt she would like to try it again, though not when his lordship was out of temper. It would be much more fun if he were enjoying it, too.

An unlikely sequel, she decided sadly as he turned to face them. The contempt in his eyes amply expressed his opinion of her.

He thought her a slut—not that she cared a groat for his opinion. Under other circumstances, she might fear for her chastity, but surely Lord Amis was too proper to seduce his father's stepdaughter in his own house.

"Miss Lydia. Webster," he said, acknowledging them curtly with a barely perceptible nod.

Lydia curtsied gracefully. In plain white India muslin, a white ribbon threaded through her hair, she was a picture of beauty, youth, and innocence. Lord Amis was manifestly unimpressed. That being so, he was unlikely to spare a second glance for Gilbert in his shabby evening coat cut down from the late Mr. Webster's. Knowing how her brother had striven with his balky neckcloth to do her credit, Ginnie was incensed all over again.

Fortunately, Reynolds came in to announce dinner. After a moment's awkward pause, Gilbert offered each of his sisters an arm and escorted them through to the dining-room. Lord Amis followed, alone, in grim silence.

Glass sparkled and silver gleamed invitingly on the spotless white cloth. Ginnie had ordered four places set at one end of the long table. She very soon wished she had placed Lord Amis at the far end, on his own.

As the soup was served, Lydia said to him with a polite smile, "I dare say you found Persia excessively interesting, my lord?"

"I dare say I might have, had I ever visited that country," he said, his sarcasm sharp enough to pierce even Lydia's armour of tranquillity. "I fear I cannot enlighten you as to the customs of Persia, as I am just returned from Russia."

Her smile faded. With a look of hurt reproach that ought to have shrivelled his cutting tongue, she applied herself to her soup.

Ginnie and Gilbert both glared at him, then set themselves to soothing their gentle sister's hurt feelings. Ginnie consulted her about the colour and style of the new gowns Judith and Priscilla needed. Gilbert ably seconded her, though as Lydia responded, his faraway look suggested that his thoughts were else-where, probably not in Buckinghamshire, Persia, or Russia, but Ancient Greece or Rome.

Lord Amis toyed with his Scotch broth as Lydia chatted happily of sleeves and skirts, full and narrow. Then the soup was followed with removes of carp stewed in port, a roast loin of pork, lamb cutlets with asparagus, scalloped potatoes, mushroom fritters, and several side dishes. Ginnie regarded the feast with sat-isfaction. The fritters, the asparagus, and the gin-gered carrots had been prepared especially to welcome home the heir. Surely such attention to his tastes must begin to win him over, to persuade him that the Web-sters were not devils incarnate.

One glance at his face disabused her of that hope. Obviously the viscount had somehow misinterpreted the lavish meal.

He must have been brooding over the imagined wrongs done to his father. Jaw set, mouth thinned to a straight line, brows meeting above his smouldering eyes and flared nostrils, the viscount stared at the laden table. As soon as Reynolds and a footman had served everyone, he dismissed them with a gesture.

Pushing back his chair, he rose to his feet and leaned on the table, glowering down at them. "As I ex-pected." He spoke with biting scorn. "Gluttons liv-ing on the fat of the land at my father's expense! Banquets, new clothes, extravagant furnishings, every luxury your covetous hearts could desire. I'll not per-mit it. There will be changes here, make no mistake!"

Lydia shrank from him and Gilbert put his arm about her shoulders. "A real Hector," he muttered.

Distantly aware of Lydia's bafflement at Gil's ref-erence to some obscure Greek or Roman, Ginnie looked up at Lord Amis and said with icy calm, "That is for the earl to decide, I believe."

"He shall soon understand how he has been duped, now that I am home to enlighten him." He slumped down in his chair again and, with his elbow on the table, leaned his forehead on the heel of his hand. "Oh, God, why did he not warn me in time for me to stop this disaster?"

"Gammon," said Gilbert the logician. "When he and Mama were married, you had just written that you expected to leave Vienna any day. He could not contact you. Besides," added Gilbert the adolescent, "he guessed you'd kick up a dust. He told me so."

Lord Amis groaned. "Even then he must have been ashamed of his weakness."

"You cannot have it both ways," Ginnie pointed out. "Lord Wooburn does not need you to enlighten him if he was already ashamed of his weakness before he married Mama. But you insult your father in calling him a dupe. He is—"

"Enough! He is an unhappy, lonely old gentleman taken advantage of by a horde of selfish, unprincipled, malicious villains!"

"Enough, indeed." Ginnie reached boiling point. "Come, Lydia, Gilbert. We shall not stay to be insulted by this self-righteous, ignorant, conceited prig."

Followed by her brother and sister, she stalked from the room with all the offended dignity at her command.

# CHAPTER THREE

"BUT I AM HUNGRY," Lydia protested as Gilbert closed the dining-room door behind them.

"It's a pity to miss such a splendid meal," he agreed, "but Ginnie's right. We couldn't have gone on eating as if nothing had been said. Bread and cheese will be nothing new."

Her eyebrows raised, Ginnie was regarding the sheepish butler, who had been lingering suspiciously close to the door.

"Shall I bring you something to the breakfast-room, miss?" he offered.

"To the day nursery, if you please, Reynolds."

Gilbert nodded. "Jove, yes, time for a council of war."

"I don't know what's come over Master Justin." The stout butler shook his head in dismay, almost in apology. "Always calm and collected and polite he was, miss, since he was in short coats. I've never seen him in such a tweak."

"I dare say it is true that those who are slowest to fly into the boughs are slowest to come down again once perched there," she said drily, already regaining her composure. "No doubt Lord Amis feels he has good reason for his outburst. You will not mention this to the servants, Reynolds."

"Certainly not, miss. I'll see something to eat is brought up right away, miss."

They went up to the day nursery at the top of the house. The long room was shabby from use, but it had an air of cleanliness and comfort. On arriving at Wooburn, Ginnie had set the maids to scrubbing and polishing the long-neglected scarred floor and battered furniture until they gleamed. The last of the evening's sun shone through spotless windows.

Colin sat at the table, writing laboriously with a stub of pencil. In her nightgown, Judith was perched on the sagging sofa, a sleepy, nightshirted twin cuddled on each side as she told them a story from Aesop. In her versions of the fables, all the animals had well-developed personalities and honourable motives.

Jack and Jimmy looked unnaturally clean and unnaturally angelic. The latter impression vanished the moment they saw Ginnie in the doorway. They sat up, instantly awake.

"Are you running away from the ogre?" Jimmy demanded.

"He'll grind your bones to make his bread," Jack suggested with ghoulish glee.

"Hush, you will wake Nathaniel and Pris." Sighing, Ginnie stepped into the room. "Colin, I asked you not to tell them those gruesome fairy tales at bedtime." She sat down opposite him, and the others joined them at the table.

He grinned. "I made sure Judith would give 'em a soothing story afterwards. What's up? Have you finished dinner already?"

"All we had was soup," Lydia said mournfully.

The twins were wide-eyed. "Is he going to starve you to death?" Jack asked.

"He had better not try!" said Colin.

"Of course he will not," Gilbert admonished his brothers. "He is a gentleman, though a deuced ill-tempered one. He insulted all of us this time, called us a horde of selfish, unprincipled, malicious villains!"

"We'll grind *his* bones to make *your* bread," Jimmy offered.

Lydia looked shocked. "Oh no, you must not do such a terrible thing."

"They don't mean it," Judith assured her, patting her hand.

"We do," Jack contradicted her.

"Of course you don't," said Ginnie firmly. The slurs Gilbert had just repeated made her blood boil anew, but she could not loose the inventive twins on their kind step-papa's only son. "However unreasonable he may be, no one is to hurt him. Promise, Jack, Jimmy."

With the greatest reluctance, they promised.

Colin frowned. "All the same, we cannot let him get away with it."

"No, we must stand up for ourselves," Gilbert agreed. Suiting action to words, he rose, his thin face serious, his slight frame stiff with resolution. "I hereby declare Justin, Lord Amis, *persona non grata*. We shall not hurt him, but we shall make him so uncomfortable he will wish he were back in Russia."

"Cut the Greek and the rest sounds good," said Colin, and the others nodded.

"Latin. It just means—"

"But Gilbert," Lydia interrupted, her forehead creased in puzzled incomprehension, a not-uncommon sight, "did you not call him Hector before?"

"No. Our stepfather always refers to him as Justin, and Reynolds... Oh!" He let out a shout of laughter. "Yes, I did call him Hector, at dinner. Hector was one of the Trojan heroes, a blustering bully of a fellow, and the word has entered the English language."

Lydia looked not one whit the wiser. The twins exchanged a meaningful glance. Ginnie felt she ought to enquire into its significance, to remind them that Lord Amis was not to be injured, but she was suddenly very tired. "Remember, Mama is to know nothing," she said, and sent them to bed. Judith went to tuck them in.

"Don't worry, Ginnie," Colin said, unexpectedly understanding. "I'll keep an eye on the brats, make sure they don't do any real harm. Ah, here comes your supper. I'm hungry again, so I'll join you. By George, you do yourselves well down there."

"I expected Mama and Step-papa to dine at home," she explained wearily, "and I ordered special treats for Lord Amis."

A procession of footmen and maids—Reynolds was far too bulky to attempt the stairs himself—bore in trays laden with covered dishes. In place of the bread and cheese and cold meat Ginnie had expected, the butler had sent up some of the food that had been on the table and most of the second course.

The senior footman leaned down to murmur in Ginnie's ear, "Mr. Reynolds said to mention that his lordship hardly touched a thing, miss."

"Indeed," said Ginnie, reviving, a militant sparkle in her eye. "I must remember to tell Cook that Lord Amis does not care for rich food. She need not go to the trouble of making any particular effort for him when the earl dines out."

JUSTIN TOOK THE DECANTER of cognac and his glass to the library. He had sat through innumerable Russian banquets, with their ceaseless toasts in vodka, brandy, and champagne, without ever letting himself become more than mellow. Tonight he had every intention of drowning his sorrows.

He looked round the room where his father had been wont to spend the best part of his time, poring over musty volumes. Here, too, were the signs of change. Silver candelabra and cherry-wood tabletops gleamed. In place of the old brown rug, a red Turkey carpet graced the floor, and matching curtains hung at the tall windows. The deep leather chairs by the fireplace were in the same style as the old ones, but a rich chestnut brown instead of the dun he recalled. Setting the decanter on an occasional table beside one of them, he sank into it to brood.

Miss Webster's words had stung, he acknowledged, pouring a second glass. What was it she had called him—a conceited prig? Presumably she did not believe him a thief or a cheat, the cant meanings of the word. Therefore she considered him a dogmatic prude, convinced of his own moral superiority and all too ready to announce it.

He had given her every reason for such an opinion, admittedly, and no reason to credit his own estimation of his superiority. Why the devil had he kissed her? Of all the bacon-brained follies, to play into her hands by lowering himself to her standards. Yet how sweet her lips had been, how silky her hair, how supple her slender body...

With a shocking disregard for its excellence, he swigged the brandy and poured another. Gazing into the topaz depths, he turned the glass between his hands.

Perhaps it was unfair of him to blame the girl and her siblings for the misdeeds of their mother. Miss Virginia Webster could not be expected to choose poverty, to reject the comforts of Wooburn just because her shameless parent had won them by foul means. In claiming to have promoted the match, she had no doubt been trying to shield her dastardly parent. He would at least give her credit for loyalty.

Yes, it was the new Lady Wooburn who was responsible for his father's misery and for exposing the Amises of Wooburn to the tattle of the ton. There must be some way to have the marriage annulled!

Setting down the empty glass, he began to pace. Lawyers, witnesses, the vicar who had performed the ceremony...if the woman had claimed widowhood when she was actually unmarried, would that rescind the sacrament and the legal contract? Of course he'd be sorry to see her children stigmatized as bastards, but his family came first. His pride and his father's happiness came first.

As he reached the end of the room and turned, the library door opened. The Earl of Wooburn stood there, lean, white-haired, slightly stooped, peering short-sightedly through his gold-rimmed spectacles.

''Father!''

A few long strides and Justin was reaching for his hand, but the earl opened his arms to take his long-absent son in a welcoming embrace.

"My dear boy!" he muttered. "My dear boy. I have missed you." He stepped back with a tremulous smile, holding Justin by both arms, and squinted at him. His spectacles had misted up. "Dash it, can't see a thing," he said and took them off.

Pulling a handkerchief from his pocket, he turned away to polish them. Justin saw him dab furtively at each corner of his eyes. Hell and the devil confound the woman who had brought the old man to tears!

"I've quit the diplomatic corps, sir," he said, pretending to have noticed nothing amiss. "My place is here at Wooburn, at your side. I mean to learn to manage the estate and to become everything you could wish for in your heir."

"My dear boy, you have always been that. Never have you caused me a moment's worry. You did not think that was why I advised you to travel?" he asked anxiously.

"Not at all, sir. You sent me to broaden my horizons."

"And did you? Broaden your horizons, I mean." The impish grin that danced across the earl's face was so unlike him that Justin dismissed it as a figment of his imagination. A momentary draught had made the candles flicker, no doubt, causing shadows to waver.

"I hope so, sir. Russia was most interesting, as was travelling back across Europe in the tsar's train."

"Ah yes, your letters from St. Petersburg and Vienna were illuminating, but I have heard nothing of your journey home. Come and sit down and tell me about it.''

Reynolds appeared as if by magic with a glass. Justin poured the cognac and told his father a little of the tsar's dash across Germany to lead his army in the Allied invasion of France. They chatted until the brass clock on the mantelpiece chimed eleven.

The earl glanced at it, set down his glass, still half full, and rose, his lean cheeks a little flushed. ''Time for me to be off,'' he said almost shyly. ''Mustn't keep a lady waiting.''

She had him completely under her thumb. No wonder he had avoided the subject of his marriage, out of sheer embarrassment. Justin tried to infuse his voice with meaning: his father could count on his support against the machinations of his wife.

''Good night, sir. I'm very glad to be home.''

''Good night, my boy. It's good to have you home. I shall present you to your new step-mama in the morning. She didn't wish to intrude tonight.''

Lady Wooburn undoubtedly hoped to put off their meeting as long as possible.

Justin watched as his father left with a jaunty step. He must feel buoyed up just to have someone on his side in the conflict. What sort of harridan had he wed?

GINNIE ENTERED her bedchamber without the usual feeling of delight. The room had not changed: the curtains of faded chintz patterned with scarlet poppies and blue cornflowers, the gleam of polished wood, the well-beaten blue rug on the floor, with the bare patch hidden under the bed, were still the same.

All her life she had longed for a room of her own, and now Lord Amis had ruined her pleasure in it.

On arriving at Wooburn she had been shocked by the dingy drabness of the mansion. "It hardly seemed worth the effort to keep things redded up," Mrs. Peaskot, the housekeeper, had said to excuse herself. "Gentlemen don't notice, and it weren't as though we ever had guests. Master Justin met his friends elsewhere so as not to disturb his lordship."

Ginnie had enjoyed supervising a thorough scrubbing and dusting and polishing, laundering and darning, washing of walls and windows, beating of carpets. The house had emerged sparkling, glowing with rich colours, redolent of beeswax and lemon oil.

The vicar's wife, Mrs. Desborough, the only lady who had always persisted in visiting the recluse, had congratulated Lady Wooburn on the change. Her ladyship had not hesitated to give her daughter the credit. Ginnie had been proud of the transformation until that odious man had accused her of living in luxury at the earl's expense.

She needed someone to confide in. The disadvantage of a room of one's own was that she could not lie in bed telling Lydia all that was on her mind. Lydia had often fallen asleep halfway through, but that had not really mattered since she understood only half of what she was told anyway. It was her sympathy and tranquil acceptance Ginnie needed.

She popped her head round the connecting door to Lydia's chamber. "Need help with the buttons, love?"

"Yes, please." The younger girl turned her back and went on plaintively, "Ginnie, I don't understand why Justin does not like us."

"You must not call him Justin, my dear." She played for time while trying to think how to explain matters to her innocent sister.

Lydia looked utterly bewildered. "His name *is* Hector, then? But why does Step-papa call him Justin?"

"Trust Gil to throw you into a confusion! His name is Justin, but you must call him Lord Amis."

"But he is our brother."

"*Step*brother. You must call him Lord Amis because he is not a real relation, and he does not wish to be related to us."

"Why does Lord Amis not like us?"

"Since he arrived at Wooburn already determined to despise us, I believe some scandalmonger in London must have told him horrid tales about us."

"Then you must explain to him."

"How can I, when the wretch is convinced of our wickedness and will not open his mouth except to revile us? He has given me no opportunity for explanations. Lyddie, promise you will not tell Gil or the others?"

"I promise I will not tell them—tell them what?"

"That Lord Amis kissed me."

"Oh, Ginnie, did he really?" Lydia squealed, her attempt to clap her hands complicating Ginnie's attempt to help her take off her chemise. "He has fallen in love with you already. How wonderfully romantic."

"Not that sort of kiss," said Ginnie sadly.

Lydia's face fell. "You mean like the sort of gentleman you warned me about, who takes advantage of young ladies? Was it perfectly horrid?"

"Well, no," she confessed. "That is why you must be particularly careful of that sort of gentleman, because it is all too easy to be taken in."

"I shall be very careful never to be alone with Lord Amis," said Lydia with a shudder.

Ginnie found the notion of Lord Amis stealing a kiss from her beautiful sister amazingly distasteful—but all too likely. "Yes, don't let him catch you alone," she said.

"What a horrid creature he is." Lydia sighed. "I thought I should like to have an older brother, but I can see I was quite mistaken."

In her nightgown of plain white cambric, she went with Ginnie back into the other chamber, helped her undress and set her ringlets in curl-papers for her. They kissed each other good-night. When she left, Ginnie sat on at the dressing-table, staring at her reflection in the mirror.

What a fright she looked in the papers, and was that a freckle on her nose? Two! Lydia never freckled. Now that Lord Amis had seen her, she would undoubtedly be the one to suffer the indignity of his advances.

The odious wretch deserved everything the twins could devise to torment him.

# CHAPTER FOUR

JUSTIN WOKE with a muzzy head and a vague feeling of uneasiness. As he lay contemplating the plaster cherubs disporting themselves with garlands on his ceiling, the events of the previous day flooded his mind.

He turned over and buried his head in the pillows, trying to hide from the memories. Lady Amabel's voice, lightly amused, telling him his father had married a slut. His father wiping away tears. His mortifying fall before Miss Webster and still more mortifying mistake in taking her for her mother. The appalling stupidity—and the seductive allurement—of that kiss.

After her first, startled reaction, she had not protested. Because she knew her brother and sister were on their way to rescue her, or because she was as depraved as her mother?

His loins stirred as he relived the moment when he had crushed her to him, her small, firm breasts against his chest, the scent of her, her mocking eyes...

How was he ever to face her with equanimity?

A brisk gallop was what he needed. He flung back the covers, rang the bell, and strode to the window to open the curtains. The early sun painted long tree-shadows across the dewy grass of the park. Breathing deep of the cool, refreshing air, he felt his head clearing. A gallop before breakfast, and then off to tackle the rapacious countess.

He went through to his dressing-room as Tebbutt arrived with hot water. Laying out his riding clothes, the valet observed, "Wouldn't know it was the same place, would you, my lord? Everything done up so nice as it is."

"At vast expense," Justin grunted, picking up his razor.

"I s'pose it would cost a fair penny," the man conceded, "hiring extra women from the village, and then a couple of new housemaids to help keep it in order. Still and all, it's no more than what his lordship can afford, and everything looks near as good as new."

"*Near* as good as new?" said his master in a strangled voice, reaching for a towel to stanch the bleeding from the nick on his chin.

"Why yes, my lord. I don't s'pose you noticed the curtain, where that pup chewed it to a shred? Mended so neat you'd never know it was tore, and they washed up nicer than I'd've expected seeing they've been hanging since your lordship moved down from the nursery. It's cold water you want on that cut, my lord, or it'll never stop bleeding. There we go. Now a spot of court plaster you can take off in a minute or two."

"Finish shaving me, will you," Justin ordered, catching sight of his unsteady hand. The whole house repaired, restored, refreshed, and he had thought it newly furnished? It seemed his father retained a modicum of control over major expenditures, at least.

He put on his drawers and hose, shirt, braces, and buckskin breeches, and tied his neckcloth in a simple knot. Snuff brown waistcoat and dark green riding coat went on next. He sat down on the stool and Tebbutt donned knit cotton gloves to help him into his top-boots, polished to a refulgent gloss since yesterday's ride from Town.

Turning the corner of the heel, his toes met an obstacle, a prickly obstacle.

"Ouch!" he shouted as Tebbutt continued trying to force the boot onto his foot. "Stop! Devil take it, there's something in there."

The valet's mouth dropped open. "In your boot, my lord?"

"Yes, damn it, in my boot. Take it off."

The obstacle followed his toes, dragging on his stocking so that it dangled from his foot by the time the boot came off. A mass of burrs was inextricably hooked into the knitted hose.

"What the devil!" Justin roared.

Tebbutt incautiously reached for the tangled jumble, pulling the stocking off Justin's foot. His glove adhered. Involuntarily, his other hand went to the rescue, and the second glove joined the collection. While he struggled to remove his hands from the gloves, Justin picked up the other boot, turned it upside down, and shook it. A cascade of burrs landed on the carpet.

Doubtless every single one promptly hooked into the pile.

Justin had to extricate his valet from the gloves. He tossed the whole conglomeration onto the dressing-table. It landed on a towel. Tebbutt moaned.

In seething silence, Justin unfastened his braces, removed his tight-legged nether garments, put on the fresh pair of stockings Tebbutt handed him, and re-donned his buckskins. In seething silence, Tebbutt found another pair of gloves, fetched another pair of boots, inspected their interiors, and helped his master put them on.

"My lord, I—"

"Not a word. I believe I know who did this." Two identical small, freckled faces, guffawing at his tumble from the saddle, rose before his inner eye. "We shall not give them the satisfaction of reacting to their prank."

Tebbutt looked at the carpet, looked at the towel, and nodded dolefully. "No, my lord."

Justin went out and galloped Prince Rurik long and hard across the fields and through the ancient pollarded forest of Burnham Beeches. All his pleasure in his return to the countryside he loved had been destroyed.

By the time he returned to the house, the breakfast room was empty, of people and of food. A footman brought him cold ham, bread, and ale, and informed him that the earl was closeted with his steward.

"And Lady Wooburn?" Justin asked.

"I think her ladyship's in the morning-room, my lord."

Deciding he'd prefer to meet the countess without his father's restraining presence, he made a quick breakfast and went to the morning room. The small, east-facing parlour was flooded with sunshine. By the window sat a small woman in a lace cap and straw-coloured gown. Beside her stood an open workbox, and concentrating on her sewing, she did not at first notice Justin's arrival.

He stood in the doorway studying her. She was in her late thirties, he judged, perhaps forty, a good twenty years younger than the earl. Fair and on the plump side, she might have been described as a cosy armful, a far cry from the dasher he had pictured. He wondered why he had expected his retiring father to have been attracted to a painted Cyprian. Nothing could be less likely, and this woman had been clever enough to realize it, hiding her true nature behind a mask of quiet domesticity.

For a moment his certainty wavered, then he recalled his father's emotional greeting. Now that she was safely wed, her debts paid, her children's future assured, the creature's behaviour in private was undoubtedly quite different from this meek pose. He was not about to let himself be deceived as the earl had been deceived.

He stepped forward and said in a harsh voice, "Lady Wooburn?"

She looked up in surprise. "You must be Lord Amis," she said with a sweet smile that was surely false after his skirmishes with her daughter yesterday. "How very glad I am that you have come home. Dear Bertie has missed you quite dreadfully."

Bertie! Never had he heard the earl referred to with such vulgar intimacy.

"My father cannot regret my absence more than I do," he snapped. "Had I been in England, he'd not have lacked the resolution to send you and your progeny to the rightabout."

Her unlined brow wrinkled in apparent puzzlement. "Progeny? I am not quite certain... Oh, do you mean prodigy? To be sure, Gilbert is amazing clever, is he not? Especially as he has had so little help with his studies since he had to leave school. But he is sixteen, you know, too old to be called a prodigy.''

While her ignorance might well be genuine, her pretence of misunderstanding infuriated him. ''I am speaking of all your offspring, madam.'' Particularly those brats who had filled his boots with burrs. ''They shall none of them profit by your wiles. You may have imposed upon my father to marry you, but your imposition shall go no further. You cannot hope to rule the roast now that I am here, you harpy!''

''Harpy?'' Her voice wavered, her mouth trembled, her eyes filled with tears.

''You are a consummate actress, madam. I have no more to say to you.'' He strode from the room, filled with righteous wrath. He was no gullible simpleton. Had she really expected to take him in with such a feeble stratagem as tears?

IN ONE OF the back sculleries, Ginnie sang as she arranged sweet peas, larkspur, phlox, and marguerite daisies in an assortment of vases. On such a beautiful morning, she could not hold resentment in her heart.

Lord Amis must have been more shaken by his fall than she had guessed, which was quite enough to account for his churlishness. She ought not to have reacted so violently. Today he'd meet Mama and realize his error and all would be well. It was a pity to be at outs with so attractive a gentleman.

''Pris, is there a nice bit of maidenhair fern left? Yes, that will do very well, thank you. Come, let us take the best of the sweet peas to the morning-room. Mama spends a great deal of time there when she cannot be with Step-papa, and she loves their fragrance so."

"Let me carry some?" Priscilla begged.

"Me, too," said Nathaniel.

Ginnie gave Priscilla the smaller of the two vases for the morning-room and persuaded Nathaniel that carrying the small, half-full, unbreakable tin watering-can was a man's task. "We must fill up the vases to the brim after we put them down," she explained.

"Flowers like lots of water," he said importantly.

"So mind you don't spill any on the way," Priscilla commanded.

The little procession marched slowly to the morning-room. A passing footman opened the door. Ginnie thanked him with a smile and went in.

She stopped in horror. By the window her mother sat with tears streaming down her woebegone face, her sewing forgotten on her lap.

"Mama!" She deposited the vase on the nearest table and ran across the room to take her mother in her arms. "Dearest Mama, what is it?"

"He called me an actress, Ginnie, and indeed I am not. I have been to the play a few times but never, ever, have I set foot on a stage."

"Of course you have not. You are speaking of Lord Amis? That gentleman jumps to a great many unwarranted conclusions!" Her smouldering ire reignited but she went on soothingly, "I dare say he meant nothing by it, Mama. A great many actresses are perfectly respectable. Think of..." She racked her brain. "Think of Mrs. Siddons."

"Oh yes!" The flow of tears ceased. "I saw Sarah Siddons once, in one of Shakespeare's plays, and though I did not understand a great deal of it, she appeared prodigious noble. If that is what Lord Amis meant, I do not mind."

"I am sure that is what he meant." Ginnie caught sight of the children's dismayed faces—and the water streaming onto the floor from vase and can. Hurriedly she went to the rescue. "It's all right, my loves. Thank you for your help. Will you go up to the schoolroom now and tell Gilbert I shall come and give you your lessons in a few minutes?"

Nodding solemnly, they departed, and she returned to her mother.

"I cannot imagine what I should do without you, Ginnie. You are such a comfort to me. Only I do think Lord Amis ought to mind his tongue, for no lady likes to be called an actress. And why did he call me a *consumptive* actress when I am perfectly healthy? Indeed, I have never felt better since I married dear Bertie, for he is so very kind and there are none of those horrid bills to worry about."

Though it was she who had done most of the worrying about the horrid bills, Ginnie let this pass. "He called you consumptive?" she asked incredulously, regarding Lady Wooburn's round, pink-cheeked face.

"Yes, and he said I was a harpy, though how he knew I used to play the harp when I was a girl I cannot guess. I was never very good at it, alas."

Ginnie had never thought to thank heaven for her mama's tenuous grasp of the English language. Considering how little she had understood of Lord Amis's tirade, it must have been chiefly his tone of voice that upset her—and that seemed to have faded from her mind already.

"I'm sure it was all a misunderstanding, Mama," she said. "I wish you will not regard it."

"I shall not," her mother said earnestly, "for I am determined to love my darling Bertie's son."

That was going altogether too far, Ginnie thought, but she nodded agreement. She saw the countess settled contentedly at her sewing again and rang for a footman to mop up the spilled water. Then she sped up to the schoolroom.

Gilbert had given up trying to teach the twins, always a thankless task, when Priscilla and Nathaniel arrived. The commotion had brought Lydia through from the day nursery, where she was pinning pieces of a shirt together at the table.

"Ginnie, they tell me Lord Amis made Mama cry?" Gilbert said, disbelieving.

"He did," Priscilla insisted.

"I saw Mama crying," Nathaniel said, his own blue eyes filling with tears. Lydia hugged him.

"He was utterly obnoxious to her," Ginnie declared. "He is a monster. The battle is on."

The twins exchanged one of their inscrutable glances. "We already started the battle," said Jack.

"Burrs in his boots," said Jimmy with deep satisfaction.

Ginnie tried to hide a grin. "Don't tell me," she said. "He is bound to complain to me sooner or later. Just remember not to do anything that will cause any injury. If you are not sure, ask Gilbert or Colin."

"I wish I could think of something," said Lydia wistfully.

"I have some good notions for you," Gilbert told her. "We shall need the twins' help. Come on, we'll talk about it in the other room."

Judith came in, late as always, for her lessons, and had to be told the story. With quiet indignation, she vowed to join the conspiracy. "I have an idea," she muttered, "but Colin will have to help."

As Ginnie set Priscilla and Nathaniel to their reading and writing, she pondered the situation. She had best not indulge in any tricks herself, she decided, since Lord Amis would probably hold her accountable for everyone else's. At most she would reinforce her orders to the servants, but she must be careful not to make them choose sides. They obeyed her willingly, and she believed they liked and respected her, yet all but the most recently hired must feel some loyalty to Lord Amis. On the other hand, she was certain that one and all adored their new mistress.

No one—except Lord Amis—ever made her gentle, amiable mother's acquaintance without growing fond of her. How dared he overset her!

He'd soon learn to regret it, she vowed.

# CHAPTER FIVE

JUSTIN CHANGED from riding clothes into morning dress and went in search of his father. He tried the steward's room first. It was empty. Through the window he saw Mills, who managed the estate, walking towards the stables deep in conversation with a tall, sturdy youth. The boy's corn gold hair suggested that he was yet another Webster, one Justin had not yet met. What the devil was he up to?

Mills was an old and trusted employee and an authoritative man. He'd not let the Websters encroach on the business of running the estate as they had in the house.

Justin wanted to talk to him about learning that business, but he would not demean himself by calling or running after them. He turned from the window and made his way to the library, his father's favourite haunt.

Gilbert looked up from his books with undisguised hostility. He was a slight, studious lad—his mother had called him "amazing clever," Justin recalled. He probably expected to be provided with a tutor, and later to be supported at a university, if his love of learning was genuine. More likely it was a pose adopted to please Lord Wooburn, a devoted reader of the classics.

Where *was* Lord Wooburn? Surely his wife had not dragged him out on yet another round of visits!

Justin finally ran his father to earth in the drawing-room. Today the visitors had come to Wooburn. They seemed perfectly at home, the long years when their host had shunned company forgotten. The earl was listening with an amused air to Squire Mason, a bluff, hearty gentleman who regarded the world as a source of funny stories. Justin remembered that before his mother died, his father used to enjoy Mason's company. At least some good had come out of the harpy's insistence on being presented to the neighbours.

And some of the neighbours appeared to have accepted her as worthy of their acquaintance. Mrs. Mason and the vicar's wife were sitting with her, chattering about whatever women chatter about.

On one of the window-seats, the second Webster daughter sat with one of the Mason girls, a pretty chit whose dark hair set off Lydia's golden beauty to great advantage. Young Mason, the squire's heir, had pulled up a chair and was gazing at her like the veriest mooncalf. So she already had a beau. Justin doubted that a mere country gentleman would satisfy her. As stepdaughter of an earl, she and her sisters must believe themselves entitled to London Seasons with all the trimmings.

They would be disappointed, Justin vowed, as would young Gilbert.

Mrs. Mason had noticed him standing in the doorway. He went to make his bows. His father and the squire joined the group and he was interrogated about Russia. Even as he spoke, he kept an eye on Lady Wooburn. She gave no sign of their earlier altercation, but behaved with a modest propriety that was altogether too good to be true. How right he had been to call her a consummate actress!

The visitors stayed for a cold collation, at which Gilbert and Virginia Webster joined them. They, too, acted in the presence of guests as if no quarrel had taken place. They treated Justin as a distant acquaintance, with politeness but without any pretence of warmth.

Justin was glad of the company to ease his first meeting with Miss Webster since he had kissed her. The general conversation distracted him from his disturbing memories and convinced him that he'd very soon be able to ignore her attractions. She was his adversary, after all. He was not the sort of man to enjoy forcing unwanted attentions on a woman he despised.

All the same, he had best avoid being alone with her, he decided. She had already once enticed him into behaving against his principles. He was the more sure it was her fault because her sister had twice the good looks, yet he had absolutely no desire to kiss the younger girl.

Virginia Webster was sitting beside the squire, listening with a smile, laughing at something he said. Justin found it all too easy to see why he had been tempted. He suspected the witch was biding her time, waiting for his father's first joy at his son's return to subside before reporting that disgraceful incident.

More callers arrived that afternoon, as word of Lord Amis's arrival spread throughout the neighbourhood. They came to welcome him home, to hear his traveller's tales, but also to see the Websters, as he could not help but notice. There was talk of picnics,

outings, fêtes, dancing assemblies, and dinner par-
ties. Lady Wooburn and her eldest daughters had
thoroughly insinuated themselves into local society.

Justin fumed silently, but found it impossible to
protest. He had known most of these people all his
life. They had stayed away from Wooburn for years in
deference to the earl's desire for solitude. Now he was
once again receiving, his son could not tell them to stay
away because he had married a woman unworthy of
their friendship. Besides, the earl was manifestly enjoying the company.

He even invited several visitors to stay and take pot
luck. Justin had no chance for private conversation
with him.

In consideration of their guests, the family did not
change for dinner, so Justin did not go up to his
chamber until the last had left. Weary from a day
spent suppressing his emotions, he donned his night-
shirt. As Tebbutt gathered up discarded clothes for
brushing, pressing, or laundering, Justin went through
to his bedchamber and climbed into bed.

"*Yeeouch!*" He popped out of bed again like a
rabbit from a hole unexpectedly inhabited by a wea-
sel. Hopping around the room, first on one foot, then
the other, he vigorously rubbed the one he wasn't
hopping on.

Tebbutt rushed in and stared. "My lord! What is
it?"

"I've been bitten," Justin howled. "Strip the bed."
He subsided into a chair, the better to rub both feet at
once. They were both breaking out into a reddish rash
that stung and itched furiously.

Pulling back top sheet and blankets, Tebbutt revealed a mass of greenery at the bottom of the bed. "Stinging nettles, my lord!"

"Those devilish twins," said his master bitterly. "The only remedy I know is dock leaves. I don't suppose you have any to hand?"

"No, my lord." Tebbutt blenched but he nobly offered, "I could take a lantern and look for some."

Justin wondered whether the beastly brats were lurking nearby, waiting to see the results of their mischief. How they would crow if he sent his valet out into the night searching for dock. He shook his head. "No, I dare say the inflammation will wear off before you could find any."

"Perhaps some sort of soothing lotion, my lord?"

"You have no more idea what to look for in the still room than I do, and I don't wish to rouse Mrs. Peaskot for such a trivial ailment. Lord, but it burns! I don't suppose you have a key to my apartments?"

"No, my lord. I expect it was lost years since, never being needed, but I'll ask Mrs. Peaskot come morning. Shall I set a footman to guard the doors, my lord, when I can't be here?"

"And have the whole damned household laughing at me? I fear once more the best we can do is to ignore the business. Those abominable children want to see me fly into the boughs and they will soon tire of their tricks if I don't. Let them think we discovered the nettles before I got into bed."

Looking dubious, Tebbutt gathered up the nettles in the bottom sheet and shook it out of the window. He remade the bed and Justin climbed back in. Already the stinging sensation in his feet was fading.

Despite the continued itching, he was tired enough to soon fall asleep.

When he woke in the morning, the grey light suggested that the spell of fine weather had come to an end. Ringing for Tebbutt, he lay back and wondered what to do about the invasion of his home.

The more he considered, the more impossible it seemed to oust the intruders. His vague hope of having the marriage annulled was an air dream. Should he succeed it would cause far more devastating a scandal than the marriage had. Worse, he was afraid his father had no desire to rid himself of the Websters. He had been shocked the previous day to see the doting glances the earl bestowed upon his bride.

She had thoroughly cozened him.

In disgust, he threw back the covers and crossed to the window. A light but steady drizzle was falling. He went through to the dressing-room as Tebbutt came in with a hot-water can in one hand and several freshly starched cravats over the other arm. Setting down the can on the marble washstand, he carefully draped the neckcloths over the back of a chair, then poured the water into the china basin.

He frowned. Testing the water with one finger, he exclaimed in puzzlement, "Stone cold! I swear the kettle was boiling, my lord, when I filled the can in the kitchen."

Justin closed his eyes and counted to ten. "Did you put it down on the way up?" he asked.

"For a moment, only a few seconds, while I picked up your lordship's neckcloths."

"Long enough, evidently, for someone to switch cans."

"I did turn my back," the valet admitted. "The twins again, my lord?"

"Possibly, but I suspect a different hand this time."

"Yes, it's not a small-boy sort of lark. More like one of the older lads." He paused, aghast, as the implications of his words sank in. "My lord, you mean all them Websters is liable to start playing tricks on us?"

About to confirm the horrid possibility, Justin recalled the impropriety of discussing the matter with his servant. However ill-bred, the Websters were now his father's family. The pranks of nine-year-olds were understandable if annoying; the involvement of their older siblings was far more unacceptable.

"No, it must have been the twins," he said with what conviction he could muster.

Tebbutt fetched more water. Justin washed and shaved, and started dressing while the valet gingerly checked his boots for nasty surprises.

Justin pulled his shirt over his head, thrusting his arms into the sleeves. Both head and hands met invisible obstructions and failed to emerge. The white linen constricted itself around his face. *"Ughffth,"* he snorted, struggling to extricate himself from the uncooperative garment.

"Don't move, my lord," begged Tebbutt, suddenly realizing his plight. "You will split a seam. There, now raise your arms if you please."

"Dammit, is that a new shirt?" Justin exploded. "We'll not go to that shirt-maker again."

"You have worn this one before, my lord," Tebbutt assured him, examining it carefully. "Look, the neckband and wristbands have been sewn together, and very neatly, too."

"Neatly?" Justin peered at the rows of tiny, straight stitches in dismay. No small boy's hand had set those stitches.

"It will take me a while to unpick without damaging the shirt, my lord."

"Devil take it, they cannot have sewn up every shirt I possess! Find me one I can wear. I'll be damned if I'll let the wretches discommode me or see me out of temper."

He bitterly regretted having lost his temper when first he met Miss Webster. Normally he prided himself on his composure, but the humiliation of his fall from Prince Rurik had shattered his self-control. If he had not shown his hand, he might have foiled the Websters without exposing himself to their malice.

With extreme caution he finished dressing, then went down to the breakfast room. Again it was empty. The sideboard held nothing but cold meat, bread, butter, and a bowl of cherries. All showed signs of having already been attacked by healthy appetites. Justin rang the bell.

One of the tan-liveried footmen appeared. "Coffee or tea, my lord?"

"Coffee. Why have all the hot dishes been removed, John?"

"Hot dishes, my lord? Miss Webster don't order none for breakfast, being as how his lordship—the earl, that is—and her ladyship breakfasts abovestairs. The young ladies only has bread and butter and tea, and a bit o' fruit they likes, too, and Master Gilbert and Master Colin makes do with cold—"

"Thank you, I do not require a detailed list of everyone's diet," said Justin. "I shall not go so far as to demand kedgeree or kidneys or kippers, but I suppose it would not be too much trouble to bring me eggs, fried ham and toast?''

"'Course not, my lord, and there's a nice bit o' beefsteak if you fancies it. Cook and Mrs. Peaskot didn't mean no harm, my lord," the chatty young man continued, "only Miss Webster said as your lordship don't care for rich foods, being as you didn't barely touch your dinner the day you come home. Likely ruined your innards in foreign parts, us reckoned in the servants' hall. They do say—''

"Enough! Nothing whatever is wrong with my digestion. Bring me coffee and the beefsteak."

Taking a handful of cherries, he sat down and gloomily consumed them. He could scarce take exception to Virginia Webster's orders when he had indeed scorned his first meal after his return to his ancestral home. Nonetheless, he'd have wagered a small fortune that concern for his digestion had not been her motive.

GINNIE WAS IN the morning-room, going over the household accounts with Mrs. Peaskot, when Lord Amis came in.

Lydia was by the window, making the best of the grey light of the rainy morning for her sewing. She actually smiled at him. Whatever she had plotted against him with Gilbert yesterday, Lydia was quite incapable of holding a grudge. However, catching Ginnie's minatory glance, she quickly concentrated on her needle once more.

Priscilla and Nathaniel, drawing pictures with coloured chalks at a small table, reacted more satisfactorily. They both stopped drawing and stared at the viscount as if he were a veritable ogre out of a fairy tale.

The housekeeper curtsied to him. "I'll come back later, shall I, miss?" she offered.

"No, don't go." Ginnie gave Lord Amis her coldest look. "I am sure his lordship will not stay long."

"I am trying to find my father," he said irritably. "He is not in the library. Do you know where he is?"

"Step-papa and Mama rarely come down before noon." To her intense annoyance, Ginnie felt a hot flush rising in her cheeks. Mama had never used to be so indolent, and one could not help wondering what she and the earl found to keep them occupied in their bedchamber all morning. Of course, they were much too old for the occupation that inevitably came to mind, yet it was impossible to ignore, throughout the day, the touches, and little caresses, and furtive kisses on the cheek.

That the same notion now dawned on Lord Amis was evidenced by his stunned expression. A touch of colour stained his cheeks, too, Ginnie was glad to see.

To avoid meeting his eye, she turned back to Mrs. Peaskot, only to find the housekeeper looking from one to the other with ill-concealed amusement. Ginnie ventured a glance at Lord Amis. Stiff with embarrassment, or outrage, he seemed to be avoiding *her* eye.

His gaze fell on Lydia and his mouth tightened. What on earth had she and Gilbert done that he recognized as her work? Ginnie wondered. Gilbert had a fertile imagination, though Lydia had none.

Ginnie was glad to be ignorant of their schemes when the viscount's attention returned to her. She faced his scrutiny with what she trusted was limpid innocence mixed with defiance—not that she cared if he did consider her responsible.

If only his crisp, light brown hair did not rouse a longing to run her fingers through it! If only she did not recall all too clearly his strong arms crushing her against his hardness, his mouth on hers, the touch of his tongue, sensitive, urgent, melting her resistance.

Unconsciously she moistened her lips. "So, you see, you will have to wait," she said abruptly.

He started. "Wait? Oh, to talk to my father. Yes, I see." His voice was slightly husky. He cleared his throat. "You are enquiring into Mrs. Peaskot's accounts, Miss Webster?"

"Mama and figures are constantly at loggerheads, sir." A fervent wish to explain to him took her by surprise. Even Gilbert did not really understand the agony she had gone through sorting out Papa's tangled finances after his death. And then had come the endless struggle to make each penny stretch further than any penny was meant to reach. Now every review of the housekeeper's neatly balanced books was a delight to her.

But Lord Amis would not sympathize if she told him. He probably thought she was searching for new ways to waste the earl's ready, or even to skim off a profit for herself.

As if reading her mind, Mrs. Peaskot said, "It's a comfort, my lord, to any honest housekeeper to have the lady of the house verify her accounts. Her late ladyship, God bless her soul, never let a week pass without doing so."

*So put that in your pipe and smoke it, you suspicious bully,* thought Ginnie smugly.

Looking disconcerted, he nodded. "I shall leave you to it, then," he said, and departed.

# CHAPTER SIX

WHEN AT LAST Justin did find his father in the library, the earl was sitting beside Gilbert, earnestly explaining some knotty point of Greek grammar. He glanced up at his son with an affectionate but absent smile.

"I'd like a word with you, sir."

"Yes, yes, my dear boy, but not just now. We are tackling a particularly difficult bit of Herodotus. I don't suppose you would be interested. Justin never was bookish," he confided to Gilbert.

"Indeed, sir," said the lad, his voice noncommittal, his eyes mocking.

"More of a sportsman—hunting, fishing, that kind of thing. Not that I didn't enjoy a good hunt in my time. I believe young Colin took out a gun after rabbits, Justin," the earl added vaguely.

"In this weather?"

White head and dark turned to the window in surprise. "It is raining! Ah yes, I remember, that is why I didn't take Emma for a drive this afternoon."

His fond tone goaded Justin into indiscretion. "I am astonished, sir, to find you so much out and about, even paying morning calls."

The earl beamed. "At first my goal was simply to make Emma comfortable by acquainting her with the neighbours, but I found myself renewing old friend-ships I had foolishly allowed to lapse. I have taken on a new lease of life, my boy. I feel ten years younger—no, twenty years!''

Though Gilbert's triumphant look made Justin fume, he was forced to say, ''I am glad to hear it, sir. I trust you will not allow your exertions to tire you.''

''Far from it.'' The old man's eyes twinkled behind his spectacles and a slight pinkness tinged his thin face.

Justin's own face burned. *That* wasn't what he had meant! So those long mornings closeted in the bed-chamber really were . . .

Miss Virginia Webster had obviously conceived the same notion, judging by her blush when she told him his father's whereabouts. Among her other faults, the chit had a thoroughly indelicate mind.

The whole family was impossible! Abandoning his father to Gilbert and Herodotus, Justin went for a long ride in the rain.

As he rode, the light drizzle gradually became a downpour. By the time he returned to Wooburn, he was soaked and chilled through. He hurried up to his chamber, rang for Tebbutt, and started stripping off his wet clothes.

''A hot bath,'' he ordered when the valet ap-peared, ''and though it may be July, this weather calls for a fire.''

Donning his dressing-gown, he paced his chamber, shivering, while he waited. Sounds of a bath being filled—the clank of buckets and swoosh of pouring water—soon came from his dressing-room. Then Tebbutt reappeared, red-faced and indignant.

"My lord, when I ordered a fire, I was told that Miss Webster has instructed that fires are to be lit only in his lordship's rooms at this season."

"What! You mean the servants obey her orders rather than mine?"

"Oh no, my lord. I put a flea in John's ear, you may be sure, and he'll be up to build a fire in the dressing room any moment, and in here, too, to take off the chill. A wood fire, being it's quicker than coal, but it'll be a few minutes afore it gives out enough heat to warm your lordship's towels."

"Just so as the bath water is hot!"

"That it is, my lord." A sudden doubt crossed Tebbutt's face. "But I'd best go and make sure." He hurried out.

Justin followed him. Steam rose from the copper tub, and the young footman was on his knees at the grate. Justin went to stand by the fireplace as crackling flames arose. John lugged his sack of wood through to the bedroom and Tebbutt closed the door to keep out draughts. He tested the water, stirred it as another footman slowly added a stream of cold, and pronounced himself satisfied.

The footman departed. Justin flung off his dressing-gown and stepped into the bath. He leaned back as the blessed heat seeped into him.

A positive paroxysm of coughs came from the bedchamber. Tebbutt went to the connecting door. As he opened it a cloud of smoke swirled through. Joining in the coughing, he slammed it shut again.

"Chimney needs sweeping," he said gloomily.

"If that's all it is." At present, Justin was unwilling to believe any misfortune accidental. "You had better go round to the other door and make sure that boy is all right.''

Tebbutt opened the door to the passage just as the footman arrived there, gasping and spluttering, his face smudged with soot, his eyes red and teary.

"There's summat blocking the chimbley," he wheezed.

"So we guessed," said Justin drily, slipping beneath the water as a cold draught hit him. "Shut the door, man. When was the chimney last swept?"

"I disremember, my lord, but Miss Webster had a fire lit to air the room afore your lordship come home, and it drawed perfect then. I done it meself."

"I knew it," Justin said with a groan.

"I put out the fire, my lord, and opened the window."

"Thank you, John, that will do. Go and wash your face." As the door closed once more behind the footman, he sat up. "We'll investigate for ourselves, Tebbutt. Where's my towel?"

"I haven't warmed it yet, my lord." The valet crossed to the washstand.

"Never mind that. I'm warm now, and this fire is burning well."

"That's odd, there's no towel here. I could swear I put out a clean one this very morning. I'll have to go to the linen cupboard, my lord."

Justin scowled. "Hurry. This water isn't growing any hotter."

Tebbutt was away an age. The water rapidly cooled. At last the valet came back, and Justin jumped out of the bath before he noticed the desperation in the man's face.

"I can't find any, my lord. There's not a one in the cupboard, nor in any of the bedchambers, neither. Not a bloody one."

"For pity's sake, *bring something,*" Justin shouted, crouching close to the fire.

A haze seeped into the dressing-room as Tebbutt dashed into the chamber and returned with the counterpane. Swathed in woodsmoke-impregnated brocade, Justin contemplated murder.

A slightly less-smoky sheet proved a more adequate substitute for a towel. Dry at last, Justin put on his dressing-gown and strode through to the bedchamber. With Tebbutt looking on, wringing his hands, he thrust his arm up the chimney and pulled down an interwoven mass of twigs, dried grass, and feathers.

"A bird's nest."

"Birds do nest in chimneys, my lord," said Tebbutt doubtfully, his unhappy gaze on the soot-blackened sleeve of the dressing-gown.

"No bird built this nest here since I informed my father of my return to England." Too high up the chimney to have been put there by the twins; unlikely to be the classical scholar or the butter-wouldn't-melt-in-her-mouth seamstress. Justin would have bet on Colin, the outdoorsman. "It is time I confronted Lady Wooburn," he announced.

"Not in your dressing-gown, my lord!" exclaimed the horrified valet.

"No, I have not quite yet taken leave of my senses. I shall dress for dinner and hope to catch her before she goes to change."

Regarding his elegant reflection in the looking-glass a short time later, he decided no one could possibly guess the disasters he had just suffered through. He appeared the cool, collected gentleman equally at home in county, London, or St. Petersburg Society. This was the imperturbable Lord Amis who was courting the beautiful, sophisticated Lady Amabel Fellowes, the Toast of the Town.

*Nothing,* he vowed, would make him lose his temper with Lady Wooburn.

He found her in the drawing-room. Though she was not alone, as he had hoped, only Lydia was with her. Lace cap and gold ringlets bowed over their eternal sewing. His aunt, too, always had a piece of embroidery about her without ever producing anything of use.

Both ladies glanced up and smiled as he entered, but Lydia's smile was suddenly snuffed out as she recalled that he was the enemy. She frowned at him.

Lady Wooburn continued to smile. "Why, Lord Amis," she said, "you are already changed for dinner. I did not realize it was so late. Lydia, we must go up." She stuck her needle into her work and started to fold it.

"I am early, ma'am. Pray wait a little, I have something to say to you." He crossed the room and leaned on the back of a chair, looking down at her sternly.

She cocked her head in enquiry, her blue eyes guileless. Lydia's frown deepened and she took her mother's hand.

"Madam, your offspring are the most disgracefully ill-bred, malicious rapscallions it has ever been my misfortune to encounter." His tone admirably even, he was about to embark upon a recital of their misdeeds when she turned to Lydia.

"Dearest," she said in a trembling voice, "does he mean he does not like you and your brothers and sisters?"

"I think so, Mama, but he will use such long words."

Tears spilling over, Lady Wooburn wailed, "But you are quite the best children anyone could ask for!"

Lydia took her in her arms and, looking back over her shoulder, said fiercely to Justin, "Go away!"

Nonplussed, he obeyed. He didn't think the girl capable of dissimulation, so her protectiveness of her mother must be genuine. That, together with his father's evident affection for the woman, and her own apparent naïvety, gave Justin a lowering feeling that he was in the wrong.

Not wrong about the situation in general, he hastened to reassure himself, but in believing Lady Wooburn the perpetrator. A memory returned to him: Virginia Webster facing him with flashing eyes and announcing, "It was not Mama but I who promoted the match, by every means in my power."

At the time, fighting in vain his urgent desire to kiss her, he had taken little note of her words. Had her mother been her cat's-paw, as well as his father?

"Where is Miss Webster?" he demanded of a passing footman.

Taken aback by his abruptness, the man stammered, "Miss Webster, my lord? I don't know for sure, my lord, but if miss ben't in the drawing-room, likely she's in the schoolroom."

Justin took the stairs two at a time. No one was in the schoolroom, but he heard voices from the day nursery beyond. He flung open the door. Half a dozen young Websters were seated around the table, about to eat. Seven pairs of eyes turned to stare.

A tall, sturdy lad who must be Colin; a flaxen-haired girl of twelve or so he hadn't seen before; the twins; the small girl and little boy who had been by the lake: all regarded him with hostile defiance. Beside the table stood Virginia, damnably desirable, damnably devious, and faintly amused.

Ginnie saw that Colin was about to speak and hushed him with a gesture. She had deliberately avoided hearing of their mischief in expectation of this moment. Whatever they had done, Lord Amis, complete to a shade in his modish evening dress, appeared to be in control of his emotions for once. Unfortunately, the chief emotion he was in control of was undoubtedly animosity. His handsome face was composed. Only his burning eyes gave him away.

She stepped forward. "My lord?"

"Miss Webster, you and your siblings have been playing childish tricks on me. I—"

"Tricks, my lord?" She widened her eyes. "What sort of tricks?"

He looked past her at the unfriendly ranks of her brothers and sisters, and suddenly she felt sorry for his discomfort.

"We can speak privately in the schoolroom," she suggested, and he stood aside to let her pass. Following, he closed the door behind him. Ginnie prudently put the scratched, ink-stained table between them. "Tricks?" she repeated.

"Burrs in my boots," he commenced.

It was the only prank she knew of, so she hastened to distract him. "Surely when you ride through the fields you are bound to pick up a burr or two sooner or later."

"Not, however, a dozen in the toe of each boot," he said sarcastically, and continued, "A bird's nest up the chimney, causing my chamber to fill with smoke. My hot shaving water replaced with cold."

"Perhaps your man set your water down for some reason and let it grow cold," Ginnie improvised, her lips beginning to twitch. What an inventive family she had! A bird's nest? That sounded like Judith, in collusion with Colin. "And birds do nest in chimneys," she pointed out.

"However, nettles do not grow between bed-sheets," he said through gritted teeth. "Nor do the necks and wrists of shirts sew themselves together."

"No," she admitted. So that was what Lydia and Gilbert had been up to. Nettles must be the twins' notion, and on the edge of acceptability; she'd have to have a word with them.

"Furthermore, this afternoon while I was taking a bath, every towel in the house miraculously vanished. How do you propose to explain *that* away?"

"Oh dear, I hope you have not caught cold!" Her immediate concern for his health faded as an indecorous vision of his plight as he emerged towelless from his bath rose in her mind, and heat in her cheeks. One way or another, she was put to the blush every time she spoke to him! She was glad of the table between them.

He, too, was flushed, whether because he wished he had not incautiously voiced his last complaint or simply with anger. Probably the latter, for his voice was cold as he said, "I await your explanation of these petty annoyances."

Ginnie matched his hauteur. "I shall endeavour to discover the culprits, Lord Amis." Not that she had any intention of chastising them. "Now, if you will excuse me, I must go and change for dinner."

With an ironic bow, he opened the door to the passage. She swept past him with her nose in the air.

On the way to her chamber, she seriously considered putting an end to the harassment. He had been quite reasonable this time, for once not letting fly with insults and unwarranted accusations, though now he had cause for reproach. He had not even demanded punishment of the offenders—possibly because he believed her one of them.

She hated being at daggers drawn with anyone, let alone a member of the household whom she must see every day. Let alone, she confessed to herself, a well-favoured, virile young gentleman.

Surely reconciliation was not impossible.

Entering her chamber, she heard Lydia moving about next door and went through. "We have no guests tonight, Lyddie. What shall you wear?"

Lydia turned to her with an utterly uncharacteristic bellicose expression. "I am sure I am too overset to care what I wear," she said dramatically. "That horrid man has made Mama cry again."

She had only the vaguest notion of what exactly Lord Amis had said, but on one point she was firm: he

had made Mama cry. If Gilbert were to bring her every
item in his lordship's wardrobe, she'd gladly sew up
every opening, buttonholes included.

Ginnie sighed. So much for reconciliation!

# CHAPTER SEVEN

"MY LORD!" Near tears, Tebbutt flung down an armful of white muslin. "Every single neckcloth we possess!"

Justin frowned down at the heap. "What is wrong with them?" he asked.

"Someone's gone and washed the starch out of 'em. They've been pressed and folded neat-like, but they're limp as dishrags, every one."

So yesterday's complaints to Lady Wooburn and her daughter had had precisely no effect. Well, it scarcely mattered if he wore a drooping cravat among such an unfashionable crew. He had noticed that Virginia and Lydia wore plain muslin gowns of the simplest cut, unadorned with ruffles and bows, in a style long since outdated. They were utterly ignorant of London modes, which now called for fuller skirts, often made of silks and sarcenets, and decorated with all sorts of fancy fal-lals.

A capital notion came to him. He'd invite Lady Amabel, and several other fashionable London friends, to stay at Wooburn for a week or two. They would help him depress the pretensions of the shabby-genteel interlopers. They'd put the Websters in their place, make them realize how far beneath the standards of the ton they fell.

Better still, Lady Amabel's stylish beauty was bound to distract him from Virginia's rustic charms.

Absently, pondering possible guests for his house party, Justin picked up one of the limp neckcloths. As Tebbutt watched in anguish, he wound it round his neck and tied it in a sad parody of the Osbaldeston knot.

Lady Amabel, however dashing, was too proper to accept a gentleman's invitation without her mother for chaperon. At present, he recalled, she was staying with the Parringales, a sophisticated youngish couple always bang up to the mark. He might as well invite them, too.

Alfred Bascom, a school friend and fellow member of White's, the epitome of the Bond Street Beau, could bring his Society-butterfly sister and her dandy husband.

Sally Jersey and Countess Lieven were high sticklers who would look down their noses at the Websters, and amusing company besides. They might be persuaded to come—but Justin did not want to give Virginia and Lydia the impression that he was trying to smooth their entrée into Almack's. No, it was best to cross the patronesses of that exclusive club off his list.

The person he really wanted to see, after his two years abroad, was George Medford; yet George was a modest fellow who was quite likely to treat the Websters as his equals. Still, Justin needed someone to confide in. And George had a sister who must be of an age to make her come-out. Let the Webster girls learn the difference between the prospects of a well-born, well-dowered sister of a marquis and a pair of dowdy social climbers.

After galloping the fidgets out of Prince Rurik, under cloudy but dry skies, Justin repaired to the breakfast room. A footman brought him buttered eggs, fried ham, muffins, and ale, and departed. Hungrily, Justin set to.

The first mouthful of eggs was somewhat overseasoned with pepper. The second took away his breath, brought tears to his eyes, and ended in a violent sneeze. Another sneeze followed, and another. Justin felt for his handkerchief, but his pockets were empty. He clapped his napkin to his face and dashed for the stairs.

Between paroxysms, he wondered by what devilish stratagem they had succeeded in waylaying his eggs between kitchen and table.

His course to his chamber was punctuated with explosions. Half blinded, he yanked open his handkerchief drawer and plunged his hand into it.

*"Oweeaaahtchoo!"* It was like picking up a handful of pins. Hastily he dropped whatever it was, mopped at his eyes, and peered into the drawer.

Two tiny, frightened black eyes peered back. A little black nose twitched at him. His own nose twitched in sympathy and another sneeze emerged, but at last the convulsions were decreasing to manageable proportions. Cautiously, he extracted a handkerchief from beneath the brown-speckled hedgehog and blew the remains of the pepper into it.

Justin studied the unhappy creature and it studied him. One of its rear legs was splinted, which had doubtless prevented its rolling into a protective ball.

*"Eek,"* said the hedgehog anxiously.

"I shan't hurt you. What I shall do to whoever put you here and caused me to rush to discover you is another matter."

"My lord?" It was, of course, Tebbutt, not the hedgehog, who spoke. "Mr. Reynolds said you... My lord! What is that dirty animal doing in your drawer?"

Closing his eyes, Justin counted swiftly to ten, then said with ironic calm, "Nothing in particular. He is as little pleased to be here as I am to find him, I collect."

"Miss Judith," said the valet with certainty. "He didn't get here on his own four legs, that's for sure, and it's Miss Judith as keeps the beasties."

"Miss Judith keeps hedgehogs?" Justin asked, incredulous.

"All manner of beasties, my lord. Down in the stables."

"Does she, indeed? I believe I shall pay a visit to the stables. Give me a neckcloth."

"A neckcloth, my lord?" Tebbutt glanced with distaste at his master's sagging cravat. "Right, my lord. I just restarched the lot, not that I suppose Miss Judith'd notice."

"For the animal! You don't think I mean to carry him in my bare hands?"

Gently cautious, he placed the little beast in the centre of the square of muslin, picked it up by the corners, and headed for the stables.

"Miss Judith?" he said curtly to the groom who came to attend him as he entered the paved yard.

The man looked alarmed. "In the loose box along aside the harness room, m'lord. Mr. Duffy, he lets miss use it for her creeturs, seeing as the stables ben't full, m'lord, an' meaning no harm. Will I fetch Mr. Duffy?''

Denying any wish to speak to the head groom, Justin strode on in the indicated direction. Most of the white-painted Dutch doors of the red brick buildings were closed, but Prince Rurik stuck his nose out of his stall and whickered a greeting.

Both top and bottom halves of the last door in the row hung open. As Justin approached, he heard the sound of muffled sobs.

He looked in. On one side of the loose box, a long trestle table held a motley assortment of crates, baskets and tin pails, from which came squeaks, snorts, chirps, caws, yowls, and the odd croak. The sobs came from a girl with a long, flaxen pigtail tied with a violet ribbon that failed to match her brown cambric gown. Her back to Justin, she was trying to shift a heavy wooden box.

"I have something of yours, I believe," he drawled.

Startled, she spun round. Her eyes were red and swollen. "You've got Prickles?" she asked eagerly.

Though he was indeed feeling decidedly prickly, he just held out the neckcloth, forbearing comment. Taking it, she knelt on the floor and opened it with great care. The hedgehog snuffled and snorted at her as she delicately stroked its spines back from head to tail.

"Oh, Prickles!" She looked up at Justin, smiling through fresh tears, then scowled and demanded, "Did you hurt him?"

"I don't think so. If I did, it was inadvertently—by accident. You should have thought of that before hiding him in my drawer."

"Oh, but that wasn't me, it was...someone else. I *told* him not to. I *told* him you might hurt Prickles. He wouldn't listen. He must have taken him when I went to collect snails."

"Snails!" Visions of drawers full of snails floated through his mind. Tebbutt would be fit for Bedlam.

"Yes, Prickles was missing when I came back. I hoped he'd just got out. I was moving things to hunt for him."

"He'd not have gone far with his leg splinted. Tell me, Miss Judith, do you doctor snails, too?"

"Heavens, no." She pulled a face. "They are for food. I hate to do it, 'cos after all I don't s'pose they care for being eaten, but Prickles likes them and so does Polyhymnia, my thrush."

"Polyhymnia? Your brother Gilbert's idea, no doubt."

"He said she was the Greek Muse of song."

"I dare say he is right. What other animals have you in your menagerie?" he asked, crossing to the table.

"It's not a menagerie." She picked up the hedgehog, put him in a decrepit basket lined with leaves, and gave him a couple of snails to crunch. "I don't keep them for people to look at. They are all sick or hurt."

"A hospital, then. Do many of your patients recover?"

"Yes, but more would if I had proper cages that let in more light and air and were easier to clean." She turned on him a steady, questioning regard from blue-grey eyes very like her eldest sister's.

"I'll see what I can do," he found himself saying. "The carpenter ought to be able to knock up something suitable if you direct him."

The grateful joy that shone in those eyes was like no expression he had ever seen in Virginia's. "Oh, *thank* you, sir," Judith cried. "That is excessively kind of you." She hesitated. "You will not tell Ginnie?"

He raised his brows. "You want to keep it secret from your sister?"

"At least until the cages are built. If you please?"

"As you wish."

"Thank you. And thank you for bringing Prickles back, my lord," she said shyly, then confessed, "It was my bird's nest up your chimney—but it was an old one. No one had lived in it this age."

"I'm glad to hear it," he assured her with due gravity, and took his leave.

Not tell Ginnie—Virginia—Miss Webster of his offer? Now why the devil not? The only reason Justin could think of was that Miss Virginia Webster would take exception to his *rapprochement* with one member of her family. Which bore out his suspicion that she was the ringleader, the instigator of all his troubles.

GINNIE FOUND her mother strolling with the earl among the formal box hedges and marble statuary of the Italian garden. They were holding hands when first she saw them, but guiltily let go as she approached along the gravel path.

Whatever the toplofty Lord Amis said, she was glad she had contrived to bring them together. Her steppapa had lost his sallowness and his melancholy, withdrawn expression. Behind his spectacles, his eyes were bright. As for Mama, she had never looked prettier, in her Pomona green gown with white lace ruffles, a broad-brimmed leghorn hat shading her happy face from the fitful noontide sunshine.

Ginnie sighed for the white lace ruffles. They'd have looked well on her own lilac muslin, but while the new countess must cut a figure for her husband's sake, his stepdaughters could claim no such necessity.

Smiling, she kissed her mother and bade her good morning, then turned to the earl. "Sir, I have one or two errands in Beaconsfield this afternoon. I know you need the carriage. May I take the gig?"

"Of course, my dear. In fact, you may do a little errand for me, if you will be so good. Yesterday's post brought a notice that the bookshop has received the books I ordered last week. I could send a groom, but if there is a volume missing, as happens not infrequently, you will be able to deal with the problem at once."

"I shall check them carefully when I pick them up. Mama, is there anything you need from the draper's, or the haberdasher's? That is where I shall chiefly be, procuring all sorts of odds and ends for Lydia. The village shop has such a limited stock."

"Yes, dear, I need a ribbon matched, and some buttons, and thread. I shall make a list before you go. You do not mean to drive the gig yourself, do you, Ginnie? I cannot like it."

"Now, Mama, surely you don't think me such a ninnyhammer! You know I have never learned to drive. I shall take a groom."

"Take Duffy," the earl advised. "He's a steady fellow, won't overset you."

"I beg your pardon." Lord Amis had approached them unnoticed. "I could not help overhearing your plans, Miss Webster. I regret to say I have urgent need of the gig this afternoon."

His smug expression informed Ginnie that his urgent need had been concocted on the spur of the moment, simply to thwart her. Catching his eye, she realized he knew she was aware of the fact. Inside, she fumed. However, she had no intention of brangling before her mama who, regarding her stepson with unwonted wariness, laid her hand on her husband's arm. The viscount would have to be allowed to win a round.

"Far be it from me to stand in your way, Lord Amis," Ginnie said untruthfully, with forced cordiality. "Doubtless your errand is more urgent than mine."

"You had best get yourself a phaeton, my boy," said the earl, "or one of these newfangled tilburies."

"I mean to replace my curricle, sir, which I sold when I went abroad."

"That's right. If you're short of the ready, just set it down to my account."

"I am not short of the ready, sir," said Lord Amis, tight-lipped.

Ginnie hid a smile as his father beamed and said proudly to his wife, "Did I not tell you, Emma, my son is a careful, sober lad? You will want horses, too, Justin. Yes, another carriage will be just the thing. I ought to have realized that we need more vehicles for a large family."

"Yes, sir," he agreed in a disgruntled tone that almost made Ginnie laugh. His purpose in purchasing a curricle was not to free a vehicle for the Websters' use. "Sir," he continued, "I have a mind to invite a few friends to stay for a week or so, if a small house party will not discommode you?"

"Not at all, not at all. A capital notion, is it not, my love?"

Lady Wooburn beamed, her mistrust vanishing. "Indeed, it will be delightful to meet your friends, Lord Amis."

Warned by his sardonic expression, Ginnie was quite certain that meeting his friends was not going to be a delightful experience. "May I enquire how many people you will invite?" she asked.

"Yes, Justin, you must consult with Virginia," the earl advised him. "The household runs so smoothly these days I sometimes forget that all is due to your efforts, my dear. You will know how many guests we can accommodate in comfort."

It was Ginnie's turn for smugness. "How many, my lord?" she persisted.

"Nine or ten."

"I dare say Mrs. Peaskot and I can manage."

"I shall give you a list when I have written the invitations. Pray excuse me now. I must go and give orders about the gig."

As he turned away, Lord Wooburn patted Ginnie's arm. "Never mind, my dear, I have no immediate need of the books you offered to fetch for me."

Lord Amis started, his stride interrupted. His ears turned red. Then he went on, leaving Ginnie feeling she had won the skirmish after all. He had the use of the gig, but only at the cost of preventing her carrying out his father's errand.

What was more, with no destination planned, he'd probably end up tooling the gig aimlessly around the country lanes for several hours. With old Patch between the shafts of the small, staid vehicle, that was a less-than-exciting occupation for an arrogant gentleman.

Silently, Ginnie wished him joy of it.

# CHAPTER EIGHT

OF ALL THE wasted afternoons! It was nearly time to change for dinner when Justin drove into the stable yard. He had deliberately stayed out late to prevent Ginnie's buying her fripperies, though he had thereby deprived his father of his books.

And all because he had stupidly challenged her for the use of the gig. Somehow the very sight of her impudent face made him lose his wits.

He had thought that at least he had won the round, until the earl mentioned the books. How she must have laughed up her sleeve! She had guessed he had no real need for the carriage, and she'd find it all too easy to hint as much to his father, making him appear childishly spiteful. Then, when the earl was disillusioned, she could go on to tell him about that damned kiss, destroying his trust in his son forever.

Gloomily, Justin entered the house.

In the front hall he met Reynolds. "Oh, there you are, my lord," said the butler. "I'll tell Cook dinner will have to be served in the dining-room. At least, I don't suppose your lordship would care to join the children for supper in the day nursery?"

"You are absolutely correct, I would not." He concealed a shudder. "Why, where is everyone?"

"An invitation from the Frobishers, my lord. An impromptu dinner party in honour of some unexpected visitors, I understand. His lordship and my lady and the two eldest Miss Websters are gone. Of course, you were also invited, my lord," he consoled, "but no one knew where you were or when you would return."

So Ginnie was gadding about, not sitting at home hoping for him to return with the gig in time for her to go to the shops. "And Mr. Gilbert?" he asked.

"Mr. Gilbert said he'd sup with the children, but I'll let him know you are back. I'm sure he'll prefer to dine with your lordship." The butler sounded distinctly dubious.

"Yes, tell him I expect to see him in the drawing-room at the usual time," Justin said sourly, recognizing a petty desire to disrupt *someone's* evening as his afternoon had been disrupted. He had not even written his invitations.

Tebbutt was waiting for him and swore that no unpleasant surprises lurked in his rooms. For once he changed without incident. He went down to the drawing-room.

No sign of Gilbert. Had the boy disregarded his summons? Reynolds uneasily announced that dinner was served.

Two places were set at one end of the long table. Justin had just sat down when Gilbert rushed in. His scarlet face testified to his haste, the Gordian knot of his cravat to the reason for it.

"I beg your pardon, my lord," he stammered, trying to smooth his hair with one hand while the other tugged at the strangling neckcloth. He managed to loosen it enough to breathe.

"Sit down," Justin grunted, and nodded to the butler.

He and Gilbert consumed the clear broth without exchanging another word. The soup was removed with rabbit stew, boiled potatoes, and a dish of green beans. Reynolds set a bowl of raspberries and a jug of cream on the table and dismissed the footman.

Justin stared at the meal. He had eaten better at a wayside inn. "What is this?" he demanded dangerously.

Gilbert smirked. "Dinner, my lord."

"I suppose this is your sister's revenge for my condemnation of her extravagance."

"You may suppose what you please."

"Oh no, my lord," said Reynolds, shocked into reckless intervention. "It's standing orders. When his lordship dines from home, Cook's to serve the simplest fare. Miss Webster reckons there's enough extra work in the kitchens with all the extra family."

"Indeed," said Justin, unable to think of any more intelligent comment. He helped himself to rabbit stew, which smelled delicious.

"If your lordship is dissatisfied..." the butler ventured.

"This will do very well for now," Justin snapped. "In future, I trust my presence at the dinner table will justify as much effort as my father's."

"To be sure, my lord."

As he ate, he brooded. Ginnie's consideration for the servants surprised him. If Gilbert had told him such a tale, he'd not have credited it for a moment, but he could not disbelieve Reynolds.

The obvious answer was that Reynolds had been misled. Without his knowledge, Ginnie was probably charging the household accounts for expensive delicacies that had never been purchased, and pocketing the difference. Only that would require Mrs. Peaskot's collusion, and Justin found it almost as difficult to suspect her of dishonesty as the butler.

Ginnie's mind was too devious for an honest man to fathom, he decided, signalling to Reynolds to refill his wineglass.

Tonight he'd write to Lady Amabel, a far more comprehensible female. Between her remaining unwed while he was in Russia, and her encouragement when he had mentioned speaking to her father, he was certain she would welcome his proposal.

In fact, she must be awaiting an offer, and his letter inviting her to Wooburn would confirm her expectations, and her parents'. He was not ready to take on new responsibilities, not until he had dealt with the Bedlam his home had become, yet on the other hand, she'd be an ally. If the house party had the effect he hoped for, he could settle down. With his wife taking over the reins of the household from Ginnie, the Websters would be firmly relegated to the status of poor relations, as they deserved.

His letter of invitation would have to be delicately worded. Best tackle it in the morning, when he had his wits about him.

In the meantime, his dinner might be plain but it was excellent. He took second helpings, noting that Gilbert was eating very little. With his nose constantly in a book, the lad probably exercised seldom. He ought to be persuaded to ride regularly—but Gilbert's health was none of Justin's affair.

"Do you play chess?" he asked abruptly. The evening had to be filled somehow.

"Yes, my lord. Do you?" Gilbert's tone verged on insolence.

"My father may have told you I am not bookish, but you'd do well to remember that does not mean I am a dunce or a simpleton," Justin retorted, piqued.

"No, my lord. I take it you wish to challenge me to a game of chess this evening?"

"I do."

"I'll be glad to accept any challenge you care to offer, my lord," said the youngster belligerently.

*Game as a bantam cock,* thought Justin, amused. Who would have thought the pale, scholarly exterior hid a spirit as pugnacious as his sister's?

He was less amused when Gilbert fought him to a draw. Unable to claim a lack of practice, for he had played a good deal in Russia, Justin had to acknowledge that young Webster possessed an impressive intellect. He almost regretted his determination to obstruct any attempt to persuade his father to pay for tutors, schools, or university.

However, his resolve was forcefully renewed when he laid his head on his pillow that night. It compressed beneath his head with a most alarming crackling noise.

Jumping out of bed, he seized the pillowcase and shook it over the floor. From it cascaded a quantity of eggshells in various stages of fragmentation.

"It could've been whole eggs," Tebbutt said, trying to look on the bright side. "It could have been *bad* eggs. These don't smell, so they must be quite fresh."

"If they smelled, you'd have removed them before I retired to bed."

Intentional or not, there was a certain clever irony in substituting eggshells for feathers, Justin realized. But the thought did not make him any happier.

"YOU MEAN Lord Amis played chess with you?" Ginnie exclaimed, stunned.

"Yes, and he played well," said Gilbert. "Pass the butter, Colin."

Colin obliged, and paused in his wolfing of a huge ham sandwich for long enough to say, "You mean you had a hard time beating him?"

"I mean the game was a draw. I'd like to play him again sometime."

"Oh Gil, never say you are going over to the enemy!"

"I want to beat him, I should have said. I shall not go so far as to ask him for another game, but I admit I enjoyed playing with a worthy opponent."

"Never mind, Ginnie," said Colin, grinning. "I shan't desert you. It's getting more difficult, with that man of his always on the watch, but the twins and I gave him a little surprise to go to bed with last night."

"Don't tell me!" Thoughtfully, she sipped her tea. "I must admit he has been amazingly restrained about all the horrid surprises he has suffered. If he complained to Step-papa, we should all be well and truly in the suds."

"If *you* complained to the earl about all the dreadful things Lord Amis has said to you and Mama, *he'd* be in the suds," Colin pointed out.

"I've no desire to be a talebearer." She could have vanquished the viscount long since by reporting to his papa the improper advances that still haunted her dreams and sent shivers down her spine. Fortunately, when in his presence she was far too busy matching wits to contemplate throwing herself into his arms. "I mean to rout him without resorting to such despicable tactics," she added.

"Apparently he has the same scruples, which is a point in his favour." Gilbert folded his napkin and stood up. "I'm off to relieve Lydia of the twins."

"Oh, Gil, can you watch Nathaniel this morning? I've arranged with Duffy to go into Beaconsfield first thing after breakfast so as to give Lord Amis no chance to requisition the gig. I shall take Priscilla, but there's not enough room for both."

"Teaching the twins is about as much as I can manage," Gilbert protested.

"Don't look at me," said Colin. "We're starting the wheat harvest on the home farm today and I wouldn't miss it for anything. Mr. Mills makes a contest of it the first day, and I must learn how he does it."

"I cannot ask Lydia to take care of Nathaniel. Both Jack and Jimmy tore their trousers shockingly yesterday—what they were up to I hate to think!—and mending them will be enough to keep her busy."

"Oh, very well," Gilbert grumbled. "I'll send Pris down to you."

Ginnie enjoyed the drive into Beaconsfield, the nearest market town, with Priscilla squeezed between her and the wiry Duffy on the gig's seat. It was still early and the air was fresh and cool. In the hedged lanes, she pointed out to her sister red and white campion, ragwort, cow parsley, and fragrant garlands of honeysuckle abuzz with bees. As they drove through the dappled shade of woodland, canopied in green and gold, the stillness and the tall, smooth, grey trunks of the beeches reminded her of Gloucester Cathedral. She wished she had more time for walking, for exploring the countryside.

At once she chided herself for complaining, even silently. Compared to the constant struggle to survive before Mama's marriage to the earl, life was bliss. She wasn't going to allow Lord Amis to spoil it.

When they reached Beaconsfield, Duffy drove the gig to the huge, half-timbered Royal Saracen's Head, at the corner of the main crossroads. He had business with a saddler in town, but he promised to be back at the inn by noon. Ginnie and Priscilla set off to do their errands.

The great open expanse in front of the inn swarmed with carriages, coaches, carts, riders, and people on foot. Shouts, neighs, barking dogs, and the crack of whips, added to rumbling wheels and the clop of hooves, made a horrid din. Here the London to Oxford highway crossed the Windsor to Aylesbury road. The Saracen's Head was not the only inn serving the traffic. The White Hart, The George, The Star, The Swan, and half a dozen smaller establishments were all busy.

Priscilla clung to Ginnie's hand and they walked close to the terraces of red-brick shops and houses that lined the street. The draper and haberdasher were on

the same side. Ginnie hoped the tumult would have
died down before they had to cross the street to the
bookseller.

They spent a long time at the draper's. Ginnie always found it difficult to decide between economy and
quality. There was no sense buying muslin at five shil-
lings a yard if it fell apart at the first washing. Yet
every time she spent a penny more of the earl's money
than was absolutely necessary, she felt a twinge of
guilt.

Colin was growing apace, and he had been too large
for years to inherit Gilbert's clothes. Though the twins
inherited from both their elder brothers, they were in-
credibly destructive. Fortunately, Nathaniel did not
mind the patched, darned garments handed down to
him.

However, Ginnie and Lydia had stopped growing,
so there were no more outgrown gowns to pass on to
Judith. Judith seemed to have shot up an inch or more
since they'd moved to Wooburn, but because she had
taken to doctoring animals, her gowns were scarce fit
to be made over for Priscilla.

Priscilla was delighted. For once she was to have a
brand-new gown. She took her time choosing.

When her primrose muslin was added to Ginnie's
purchases, the heap was alarmingly large. The new
assistant who had helped them looked at her askance
when she ordered the bill sent to Lord Wooburn, but
the proprietor knew her by now. If she chose to dress
in as old-fashioned a manner as a Quaker, that was her
affair. Straight skirts without trimmings used less cloth
than the new modes, but the size of her family guar-

anteed good profits. He promised to have the stuffs wrapped and delivered to The Saracen's Head.

The matching of buttons and ribbons at the haberdasher's was also a lengthy business. Priscilla whined for an expensive silk rose for her bonnet, one Ginnie would have liked for herself had it not cost a whole half-crown. At last she finished and, her basket crammed full of odds and ends, they returned along the hot, dusty street to the inn.

As they entered the inn yard, Ginnie saw a familiar figure coming out of the Receiving Office. Lord Amis must have ridden into town to post his invitations. Of course he had the right to invite guests, but no gentleman could possibly realize how much extra work it meant. Hot and tired as she was, if she met him face to face she'd likely tell him. She pulled Priscilla aside into a shadowed corner, and he passed without seeing them.

"I want to go home now," said Priscilla as Ginnie unloaded her basket into the gig's boot.

"I have to collect Step-papa's books."

"If you had not hidden from Lord Amis, you could have asked him to fetch them."

"We are not on such terms with Lord Amis that I should ever ask a favour of him. Come on, it will only take us a few minutes."

"I'm tired. I'll wait here for you."

Ginnie looked around at the confusion of horses, carriages, ostlers, coachmen, and travellers. "I cannot let you wait here alone."

Priscilla pouted. "Lord Amis would have waited with me if you had not hidden from him."

"Damn Lord Amis! I mean, bother Lord Amis. Anyway, he is so disagreeable I dare say he would not have. Don't let him make us quarrel." She felt her purse. "Stop grumbling and I'll buy you a penny bun."

"With icing and currants?"

"With icing and currants." Taking her sister's hand in a firm grip, Ginnie made for the street.

A momentary lull in the stream of vehicles allowed them to cross to the bookshop without difficulty. Lord Wooburn had ordered two works, but one had five volumes and the other six. Ginnie examined them carefully. All were present and correct. The bookseller wrapped them in two brown-paper parcels tied with string. When he put them in her basket, they felt as heavy as a millstone.

She needed both hands to carry the basket. "Hold tight on to my skirt while we cross the road," she ordered Priscilla.

"But there's a pastry-cook's just two doors down."

All she wanted to do was rid herself of the millstone. "There's another right by the inn," she said.

"They might not have—"

"Come *on!*"

The bustle in the street had increased again. Dodging a hay wagon, a stagecoach, and a speeding whiskey, Ginnie made it to the other side. She glanced down to point out the bow-windowed confectioner's shop to her sister. Priscilla was not there.

# CHAPTER NINE

AGHAST, Ginnie whirled round and scanned the street, dreading to see a small crumpled body under hoof or wheel.

Traffic moved on smoothly in both directions. Her heart's pounding quieted a little as she realized there was no commotion indicating an accident. The dratted child was probably gawking at the confectioner's display.

She stood on tiptoe, trying to see over six huge shire-horses pulling a heavy dray. At last it passed. Wearily she hefted her laden basket, ready to cross again, when she saw Priscilla skipping towards her, holding the hand of a youngish gentleman.

On the short side, and plump, he wore a sky-blue coat with padded shoulders, dazzling yellow inexpressibles, curly brimmed beaver, and glossy, gold-tasselled topboots. His neckcloth and shirt points were of such a height he was forced to tilt his head back and look down his nose to see straight ahead. Ginnie wondered how he had ever managed to notice her little sister.

"Ginnie, this is Sir William," Priscilla called as they approached. "He asked me if I was with you, and then he helped me to cross."

"Always happy to oblige a lovely lady, ma'am," said Sir William, bowing as far as his neckcloth permitted.

The admiring gleam in his eye told Ginnie he was referring to her, not her sister. He must have seen them together before he offered his assistance. Amused and a little flattered, she thanked him.

"Allow me to carry your basket, ma'am," he offered gallantly.

"Thank you, sir, but we are only going as far as The Saracen's Head."

"And the pastry-cook's," Priscilla reminded her.

"Any distance is too far." He took the basket. Ginnie's arms were tired, so she made no further protest, but took Priscilla's hand and proceeded towards the shop. At her side, Sir William continued, "I must and will be permitted to treat you both to a dish of tea."

Tea sounded like heaven, but Ginnie politely declined. No respectable female would accept an invitation from a stranger. In the shop, she would not even let him pay for Priscilla's penny bun. Though he looked a little sulky, he refused to hand over the basket when she tried to take it back. Rather than indulge in an undignified scuffle, she let him carry it towards the inn.

"Do you live in Beaconsfield, ma'am?" he asked as they reached the archway to the yard.

"A little distance outside, sir."

"I'm just passing through, driving up to Town. I'll tell you what, I don't mind if I stop here for the night if you'll join me."

Outraged, she glared at him and seized the basket. "I must have misheard!" she exclaimed.

"For dinner, ma'am, for dinner," he said hastily. He then proceeded to give this disclaimer the lie when he seized her by the shoulders and attempted to plant a kiss on her lips.

That he missed was due as much to the basket and his cravat as to her instant reaction in turning her head. She felt the brim of her straw bonnet scrape across his face and hoped it had scratched him thoroughly.

"*Grawkh-kh-kh!*" he uttered.

For a moment she assumed with satisfaction that his neckcloth was strangling him, until she looked back and saw that Lord Amis had him by the collar, shaking him till his teeth rattled.

Whether Sir William's face was redder than her own, she'd not have cared to wager.

Lord Amis dropped the unfortunate fellow, dismissed him with a jerk of the head, and turned his grim gaze on Ginnie. The neat propriety of his dress made the other appear a foppish demi-beau. On the whole, she thought she had best thank him for his intervention, though she had been perfectly capable of sending Sir William to the rightabout.

That popinjay was slinking away, muttering apologies. At the same moment, Ginnie realized that Priscilla was clinging to her in fright and Lord Amis realized that several interested spectators had gathered. His cold, haughty glance sent them scurrying about their business. She shifted the basket to one arm and put the other comfortingly about her sister's shoulders.

"You must expect to be accosted by scoundrels, Miss Webster, if you choose to walk about the streets without your maid." His voice was no less disdainful for being soft.

She raised her chin. "I have no maid, Lord Amis."

He looked taken aback, but quickly rallied. "A footman, then."

"I defy you to have fitted one more person in the gig."

"At least the groom!"

"The earl advised me to have Duffy drive us, and he had business of his own in Beaconsfield. I could not ask him to attend my every step. I was managing perfectly well on my own, I assure you."

His smile was contemptuous. "Ah yes, I should have guessed you welcomed that coxcomb's attentions. I saw you coming out of the confectioner's with him. No respectable female allows a stranger to treat her."

"He wasn't a stranger," Priscilla piped up indignantly. "*He* was a nice man. He helped me cross the street."

"And *he* offered to carry my basket," said Ginnie. Her arm was leaden. She set down the basket with a thump. She did not precisely intend it to land on Lord Amis's toes.

He yelped. "What the devil have you got in there? Have you bought up the jeweller's entire stock?" Stooping, he picked it up.

"Your father's books," she said coldly, taking it from him. "Now, if you will excuse us, I shall find Duffy and go home. I am more than ready for my luncheon, since I did *not* allow Sir William to treat us."

"He didn't even pay for my bun," Priscilla added stoutly.

Smiling at the viscount's discomfiture, Ginnie turned towards the inn door. At that moment, an apprentice from the draper's rushed up, his arms piled with bulky packages, anchored by his chin.

"Miss, oh miss, what'll I do wi' your stuffs?"

"Take them round to the yard and ask for Lord Wooburn's gig," she instructed him. "I shall be there in a moment."

From behind her came Lord Amis's sarcastic voice. "Not the jeweller's entire stock, but the draper's."

Ignoring him, she bustled Priscilla into the inn. She asked a waiter to find Duffy in the taproom and send him to the gig. As she and Priscilla made their way out to the yard, she blinked away stinging tears. Lord Amis was determined to think the worst of her, and nothing she could say or do would change his mind.

TRUTH TO TELL, Justin was a little ashamed of himself. However much he disbelieved Ginnie, Priscilla's remark about her bun had rung true, and those devilish heavy parcels probably *had* contained his father's books.

Flexing his bruised toes, he reminded himself of the vast quantity of purchases the girls had made at the draper's, certainly on the earl's account. And he had found Miss Webster in a stranger's embrace, in the public street. If she truly objected to the man's attentions, why had she not thanked him for coming to the rescue?

Seeing the fellow assault her had made his blood boil, he admitted gloomily as he headed for the coffee room. He had no right to condemn a man for something he himself had done not so long ago, but he had been as mad as a hornet. If the dandy had not capitulated at once, he would have knocked him down. Anyone might be excused for suspecting jealousy—though that was nonsense, of course. One could not be jealous of a female one disliked and despised.

He sat down at a table and a waiter sped to serve him. His appetite had deserted him. He had been about to offer Miss Webster and the child refreshments when the boy had arrived with her purchases—thank heaven. He could just imagine how she'd have responded.

*"Thank you, my lord, but if one should not allow a stranger to treat one, how much less should one accept favours from an enemy."* She would doubtless have refused with something on those lines; he could almost hear her mocking voice.

Ordering ale, he drank it quickly and went out to retrieve Prince Rurik from the stables. As he rode cross-country homeward, he wondered again why Virginia had not yet reported his stolen kiss to his father. Then a dreadful possibility struck him: had she forgotten it? Had the moment that was branded on his memory been so unimportant to her that it had slipped from her mind? Was he so inept a lover?

Pride rebelled. Either she was so practised a Paphian that the most expert kiss meant nothing to her, or she had laid some deep, dark plot for his destruction.

He reached the home farm and was cantering through a cherry orchard when he heard howls of childish distress. Reining in, he glanced about. The littlest Webster boy stood under a tree, holding one wrist in the other hand. Tears rolled down his crimson face from screwed-shut eyes, and from his open mouth came the piercing, terrified wails.

Justin sprang from the saddle, leaving Prince Rurik to wander. A few strides took him to the child and he gathered him in his arms.

"What is wrong? What's the matter?" Damn it, what was his name? Nathan—no, Nathaniel.

"A waps stinged me," Nathaniel whimpered, already soothed by the presence of a grown-up. He held out his hand, showing the red swelling on the palm. "It hurts."

"I know, a wasp sting hurts like the very... badly." Justin took the little hand in his and examined it gravely. "If you are brave enough, I'll take you home on my big horse. Your nurse will know how to make it better."

The boy gazed up at him with huge, tear-drenched blue eyes. "I want to go on your horse, please, sir, but I don't got a nurse."

"Your governess, then." Justin picked him up and carried him to where Prince Rurik cropped the grass.

"What's a gov'ess?"

Good Lord, the child was as dim-witted as his mother. "The lady who teaches you and looks after you," he said. Mounting, he reached down, caught Nathaniel under the arms, and swung him up before him. He started Prince Rurik off at a gentle amble.

"Ginnie teaches me, but she's my sister, not a gov'ess. I can write all my ABCs. 'Cept I sometimes get them backwards."

"Ginnie teaches you?" he asked, disconcerted. "Who takes care of you?"

"Ginnie an' Lydia an' Gilbert an' Colin takes turns, an' Judif sometimes, but Judif can't make the twins be good 'cos they're too naughty."

"No nursemaid? No nursemaid," he concluded as Nathaniel looked blank. "Who is supposed to be watching you now?"

"Gilbert, 'cos Ginnie went to shopping. There wasn't room for me," he added sadly.

"What was Gilbert about to let you wander alone so far from the house?"

"He was teaching the twins. They're ever so naughty, like I said. He forgetted me. So I runned away to catch a waps to put in your room to sting you. But it stinged me instead." His mouth wobbled. "It still hurts."

Justin winced. "We are nearly home." He turned into the track that led to the stables. "Why did you want the wasp to sting me? It would have hurt me, too."

"You said horrid things to Ginnie and you made Mama cry," the child accused. "I didn't 'member it hurted so bad. Ginnie said we mustn't hurt you, just make you go back to Russia."

"I see." He didn't, quite. Lady Wooburn might believe he could be chased back to Russia, but Virginia was not so naïve.

At least she had ruled out injuring him. Thinking back, he realized how much worse his sufferings could have been. Broken glass in his boots, a rat or an adder in his drawer, clothes ripped instead of sewn up, brambles in his bed . . . He grimaced. *Comparatively,* he had much to be thankful for.

Then there was the matter of no governess, no nurse, no abigail, and he recalled Tebbutt speaking of just a couple of extra housemaids. Had he misjudged Virginia? More likely he had misjudged his father's ability to prevent his new family from taking advantage of him.

As they came in sight of the house, a flood of people poured out into the gardens. Gilbert led the way, followed by Lydia and the twins. Behind them came the servants, housemaids in caps and aprons, footmen in livery, Mrs. Peaskot, stout Reynolds puffing in the rear. As Judith and a pair of grooms ran from the stables, Justin scanned the house for signs of smoke or flame.

Hanging on to Nathaniel, he stood up in the stirrups and called, "What is it? Fire?"

Heads swung his way. "There he is!" screeched one of the maids.

Gilbert, Lydia, Judith, and the housekeeper converged on Prince Rurik, who tossed his head nervously. The twins made good their escape from lessons, and Reynolds ushered the servants back into the house. Justin presumed it was not burning down.

"Oh, Nathaniel!" Lydia sobbed, casting a reproachful glance at Justin.

"Where did you take him?" Gilbert demanded, reaching up to lift his little brother down.

"Far from taking him anywhere, I found him and brought him home," said Justin, righteously indignant.

"I got stinged by a waps," Nathaniel. announced proudly, displaying his hand. Though the stung area was red and swollen, his tears had dried so the pain must have eased.

"What you need is a spot of sal volatile on that, Master Nathaniel," the housekeeper said with welcome practicality. "Bring him along to my room, Master Gilbert."

Gilbert picked him up, his slight frame staggering a trifle beneath the weight of the sturdy four-year-old. He followed Mrs. Peaskot, and Lydia trailed after them, wiping her eyes.

Justin set Prince Rurik in motion. Judith walked beside him towards the stables, unafraid of the great stallion towering over her.

"Gilbert ought to have thanked you, my lord," she said earnestly. "He was too upset by Nathaniel disappearing to have his wits about him."

"No matter."

"But *I* thank you for bringing him home. And for sending the carpenter to help me. He has already started work on the cages."

"Good."

They continued a little way in silence, then she burst out, "You are so kind, I don't understand why you made Mama cry."

His cheeks burned. "That was a mistake," he told her, looking straight ahead.

"I knew it must be. She is so gentle and amiable, no one could dislike her."

They entered the stable yard and Justin dismounted. Judith rubbed Prince Rurik's nose and fed him a sugar lump from the pocket of her grubby gown. She really had a way with animals, large and small.

She was an endearing child, Justin thought as he entered the house. The younger Websters shouldn't have to suffer because of his quarrel with their sister. Perhaps he should try to persuade his father that not to hire a nurse and a governess was a false economy. If the children were not properly brought up and educated, they'd only cause trouble later.

The elder Websters were another matter altogether. They were old enough to be held accountable for their misdeeds. He must ensure that the earl did not offer to provide for the boys' schooling, nor for London Seasons for the young ladies, let alone dowries.

# CHAPTER TEN

WHEN JUSTIN WENT down after changing out of his riding clothes, the earl was in the morning-room, reading to his countess as she sewed. Justin recognized Pope's translation of the *Iliad*. She probably understood not one word in three, but both appeared contented.

Here on the east side of the house, they must have missed all the excitement of the search for Nathaniel. He had no intention of telling them. The wasp sting had been punishment enough for the little boy's escapade.

They both smiled as he joined them, his father with affection, Lady Wooburn with the sweet amiability he had thought a pose. Now he was prepared to believe that Virginia Webster had led her mother by the nose as well as his father. She was an abominably managing female.

At least he could make sure that her influence over her younger siblings was obstructed.

"Sir, I have just discovered that the children have neither nurse nor governess."

The earl looked startled. "Have they not, my boy? How very remiss."

"I do feel some care should be taken for their education and discipline."

"But of course!" He turned to his wife. "My dear, did I not overhear Mrs. Mason regretting the necessity of turning off their governess because the youngest chit is too old for the schoolroom?"

"Yes, Bertie. She told me Miss Tullycombe has been a veri... a veri-something treasure. And Lady Rill mentioned that their old nurse—although she is not really so very old, only they pensioned her off because the boys are grown, but they all visit her constantly because she is a prodigious *comfortable* woman—and Lady Rill says she finds life shockingly dull without children about her, so perhaps she will like to come and look after my darlings?"

Her husband patted her plump little hand, his fond gaze fixed on her face. "I dare say she will," he said vaguely. "Justin, may I leave it to you to arrange everything?"

"Certainly, sir." Excellent! Miss Webster would have no say in the business. "There is another matter," he went on, though far from sure he had his father's attention. "I cannot help thinking it would be most unwise to spoil the older youngsters by overindulgence. It would be a mistake to let Miss Webster and Miss Lydia believe they are entitled to make their come-outs in Society and to be furnished with marriage portions."

A movement at the doorway caught his eye. Virginia stood there, her outraged expression indicating she had heard his words.

"Nor," he continued smoothly, "is it at all necessary to provide Colin and Gilbert with tutors."

The earl turned to him, suddenly alert. "My dear boy, you are quite right. Gilbert must most certainly have a tutor. I cannot imagine how I have been so neglectful of my duties. To be sure I have been teaching him a little myself, but he needs someone better versed in explaining the intricacies of grammar. He ought to be preparing for the university.''

''But, sir—''

''What else was it you were saying? Colin—now there I believe you are wrong. Young Colin has no desire for a classical education. But the girls, yes, yes, they must be presented at Court, of course, and go to balls and suchlike gadding about. Husband-hunting is the business of young women. As for their portions, I shall send for my lawyer at once.''

Ginnie gave Justin a triumphant smile and left.

''Sir, I...'' he started to protest, but his father was addressing Lady Wooburn.

''My dear Emma,'' he said reproachfully, ''why have you never drawn my attention to my negligence? That your children should lack for anything is most distressing.''

''Oh, Bertie, you have been so very generous to us!'' The countess had tears in her eyes. ''Giving all my darlings a home! Though of course I could not have married you otherwise. But Ginnie told me you even paid those horrid debts she was always worrying about. She said we must not take advantage of your muni... muni...kindness, and she forbade me to mention balls and gowns and *frivolous* things.''

''You have an admirable daughter, my love, almost as admirable as her mother.'' He squeezed her hand. ''But I am very well to pass, you know, and well able to provide every advantage to my new family.''

''Oh, Bertie!'' Lady Wooburn sighed.

They had forgotten Justin's presence so he took himself off. In the doorway he almost stumbled over Virginia's basket. The two parcels of books were in it, a vivid reminder that all was not always what it seemed.

He picked up the basket and returned to set it on the floor beside his father. The earl tore himself away from the sweet nothings he was murmuring in his lady's ear for long enough to glance up and murmur absently, "Thank you, my boy."

Justin departed in a very thoughtful mood.

His plan had gone awry, had had precisely the opposite effect to that he had intended. Yet he could not be sorry. If Ginnie had truly forbidden her family to take advantage of the earl's munificence—that was surely the word her ladyship had sought in vain, he thought with an indulgent smile—then he had misinterpreted her motives ever since he came home.

He did not doubt that she had contrived the marriage, but his disapproval was pointless since his father doted on his bride and was happier than he had been for years. Miss Webster had insinuated her penniless family into a comfortable home, and then done her best to minimize the inevitable disruption of a household faced with ten new members.

Justin recalled how bright and cheerful the house had seemed on his arrival. Not extravagant expenditure, as he had assumed, but simply someone in charge who cared, and who knew how to keep the servants to their work. To the staff, as to her family, Miss Webster's word was law.

Even when it came to feeding the heir to the earl-dom on rabbit stew and boiled potatoes, he remembered with a rueful grin.

The earl and countess were present for luncheon, which was therefore a tempting array of cold dishes set out in the breakfast room. In their presence, the usual truce prevailed. The Websters were as unwilling as Justin to let Lord and Lady Wooburn discover the animosity between them.

Though Justin was almost ready to let bygones be bygones, Virginia's demeanour made it quite plain she had no such intention. Indeed she had renewed reasons for resentment. Only that morning he had once more virtually accused her of being a lightskirt, and then gone on to attempt to destroy her chances of making a good match.

He had been mistaken, but after the tricks played on him, he was by no means prepared to apologize. He ignored her, insofar as it was possible for any red-blooded young man to ignore so delectable a face and figure.

As he ate, he became aware that Gilbert was sending him pleading glances whenever his eldest sister was otherwise occupied. Intrigued, he lingered over a red-currant tart, which in truth was worthy of being lingered over. Gilbert, whose appetite was small, had more difficulty in making his meal last, but he stretched a cup of coffee until everyone else finished and departed.

"Well?"

"Sir, I must thank you for rescuing Nathaniel." The lad pushed away his cup of coffee, stone-cold by now. "He told me all about it."

"Even how he planned to put a 'waps' in my chamber?" Justin asked drily.

"Yes, sir. I told him that wasn't on. It was excessively noble of you to overlook it and bring him home."

"He's naught but a little child misled by his elders."

Gilbert's thin face crimsoned. "I have tried to keep the pranks from getting out of hand, sir. Ginnie didn't want to know the details so she told me to make sure you were not hurt."

"Then she doesn't know who was responsible for which?" He held up his hand as Gilbert started to speak. "No, I've no wish to hear your confession."

"I think it's time it all stopped, sir."

"I'm gratified to hear it. I trust you can persuade your siblings to agree."

"I'll try. Please, you won't tell Ginnie I let Nathaniel run off alone, will you?"

"Is your sister such an ogre?" Justin asked with considerable curiosity.

Gilbert looked stunned. "An ogre? *Ginnie?* Lord, no! Only she has enough to worry about without thinking I can't be trusted to look after the children. I'll never let it happen again," he said anxiously. "You won't tell her, will you?"

"Mum's the word," he promised.

"Oh, thank you, sir. If you want another game of chess sometime, just let me know."

"Thank you, I shall," said Justin, hiding a smile.

Jubilant, Gilbert went off, to the library, no doubt. So scholarly a youth ought not to be wasting his time taking care of small children, Justin decided. He'd drive over to the Masons' that very afternoon, to make enquiries about their cast-off governess.

The trouble was, Miss Webster would never believe hiring a governess and a nurse was his own idea. She'd be convinced his father had forced him to do it, and he couldn't blame her.

THE EUPHORIA of witnessing Lord Amis hoist with his own petard had faded. Climbing the stairs to the schoolroom, Ginnie pondered the depth of detestation that had led him to his failed attempt to deprive her and her family of the fruits of Mama's marriage.

How he must hate them all to let his father see his malice! Fortunately, dear Step-papa was too vague and too charitable to understand his purpose. Lord Amis had brought about precisely the opposite of what he had intended.

Though Ginnie would never have lowered herself to request such favours, the prospect of a tutor for Gilbert and a Season for herself and Lydia had delighted her. A few moments of reflection had diminished her delight. She was glad for Gil and Lydia, of course, but she herself could not possibly be spared from Wooburn, especially without their help in caring for the younger children. For her, the dream of a Season was as far off as ever.

And she *had* dreamed, of balls and modish clothes and meeting a gentleman she could love and respect, who loved her with all his heart. To no one in the world would she have confessed the fact that that gentleman had recently taken on the lineaments of the abominable Lord Amis.

In her dreams he did not scowl and scold. In her dreams he was tender and passionate, and his eyes told her she was the most desirable woman in the world.

She reached the schoolroom and returned to reality with a thud.

The twins had gone off about whatever it was they found to do in the Wooburn park. Thank heaven the summer continued fine. Keeping them amused indoors in bad weather was always a nightmare. Come winter, at their age, they really ought to spend more time at their lessons, but it wouldn't be fair to Gilbert to expect him to neglect his own studies.

Judith, Priscilla, and Nathaniel awaited her. Nathaniel was bursting with news.

"A waps stung me," he said proudly. He offered his hand for Ginnie's inspection.

There was a reddish bump with a darker pinpoint in the centre. "Is it all better now?" she asked.

"Nearly. Mrs. Peasocks put stuff on it. Lord Amis brung me home on Prince Rook."

"Brought. Lord Amis *what?*"

"He gave me a ride on his big horse. He was nice."

"He may've been nice to you," said Priscilla hotly, "but he was horrid to Ginnie again when we met him in Beaconsfield this morning."

"He has been kind to me, too," Judith said, her voice tentative. "Kind *and* helpful, to me and the animals."

"What has he done to help?" Ginnie demanded, in her astonishment forgetting to ask where Lord Amis had brought Nathaniel home from.

Judith looked down at the table. "I wasn't going to tell you, because I know you'll be cross as a bear at a stake."

"Judith Webster, what have you been up to?"

"Nothing! Honestly, I never asked for anything. I just happened to mention that it would be easier to take care of the animals if they had proper cages...and he told the estate carpenter to make some."

"I see." She had no right to criticize her sister, when she was ready to accept London Seasons and dowries and tutors, though from the earl, not his supercilious son. "You are quite sure you did not request them? Then how on earth did the subject ever come up?"

"That beast Colin took my hedgehog to put in Lord Amis's drawer. I told him not to. I told him poor Prickles was bound to get hurt, and he already has a broken leg. But Lord Amis didn't hurt him at all. He brought him back to me, so you see he really is kind. At least sometimes."

Ginnie's mind was awhirl. The viscount had certainly been kind to her brother and sister. She found it hard to believe his kindness was entirely altruistic. More likely he had some devious plan to rob her of her allies.

His conduct that morning had made it absolutely clear that towards her he had not softened in the slightest.

# CHAPTER ELEVEN

THE WEATHER continuing fine, the Frobishers invited their neighbours to a picnic at Burnham Beeches. Children of all ages were included in the invitation.

"Many of those old trees are hollow," the Honourable Mrs. Frobisher explained to Ginnie. "My children have such fun climbing and exploring, and I know your brothers and sisters will too."

Ginnie refrained from pointing out to the friendly young matron that the Frobisher offspring had nurses and nursemaids galore to supervise their explorations. She politely agreed that it sounded like a wonderful place for a picnic, but she didn't expect to have the leisure to enjoy the outing.

That was before the new governess arrived and, a day later, the Rills' old nurse, accompanied by a fresh-faced niece whose sole duty would be to wait upon the nursery.

At first Ginnie was reluctant to allow anyone else to take charge of her siblings. Then she talked to Mrs. Mason and to Lady Rill. She spent the first day in the schoolroom watching over Miss Tullycombe's shoulder.

The governess was equally capable at teaching Nathaniel his alphabet and Judith French and ladylike deportment. She even seemed able to persuade Jack and Jimmy to concentrate on their studies, though the twins grumbled heartily. The nursemaid, Alice, was cheerful and willing. As for Nurse, as soon as Nathaniel confided that the plump, grey-haired woman had a "comf'able" lap, Ginnie knew she would do admirably.

So Ginnie wholeheartedly thanked Lord Wooburn for hiring the three.

"It's not me you need to thank, my dear," he told her. "The whole thing was Justin's notion. Truth to tell, I'm ashamed to say, I didn't even realize you had no governess until he pointed it out to me."

With the intention of ensuring they never did have a governess, Ginnie was certain. As with the business of Seasons and dowries and a tutor for Gilbert, Lord Amis's mischief had misfired. She did not express her gratitude to the viscount.

Nonetheless, she was able to look forward to the picnic with unalloyed pleasure, knowing Alice would be there to superintend Nathaniel and Priscilla. The twins, active and sturdy, were unlikely to come to grief as long as she impressed upon them not to go out of sight, or at least sound, of the other picnickers. If she worried about those two breaking the odd leg or arm, she'd never get a moment's peace.

The day before the picnic, Lord Amis bought a curricle, navy with daffodil trim, and a handsome team of greys. Ginnie was taken aback when he invited Gilbert to drive to Burnham Beeches with him in the dashing equipage. When Gilbert eagerly accepted, she was dismayed.

Colin explained their brother's capitulation. "It stands to reason only a nodcock would refuse a ride in such a bang-up rig," he said enviously. "And those cattle are prime bits of blood and bone. Sixteen-mile-an-hour tits, I shouldn't wonder."

His envy was assuaged when Lord Amis, after briefly consulting Mills, suggested that Colin drive the gig to the picnic. Old Patch was not a patch on the greys, but he'd be handling the ribbons himself, and he'd never before driven anything more exciting than a farm cart.

Ginnie's suspicions were *not* assuaged. It appeared more and more as if Lord Amis were resolved to win over her brothers and sisters, leaving her alone to defend her family against his machinations.

On the other hand, it made sense for Colin to drive the gig, with her and Nathaniel as his passengers. Otherwise, even with Lydia taken up by young Mr. Mason in his whiskey, they'd be hard-pressed to fit everyone into the carriage.

The day of the picnic dawned with the sort of wispy mist that often presages a glorious day. Helping Lydia dress in a gown of speedwell blue to match her eyes, Ginnie made up her mind to take a holiday from all her worries and enjoy herself. She chose a walking dress of deep rose cambric muslin, bound at the high waist with a white sash. Regarding herself and her sister in the looking-glass, she decided the simplicity of their gowns was elegant, if not in the latest mode.

Smiling, she hugged Lydia. "You are a sight to turn Peter Mason's head, if it were not already turned. He is a steady young man, I believe, but make sure he does not allow his whiskey to become separated from the other carriages."

"I shall. He might try to kiss me and I should hate to have to be cross with a friend," said Lydia placidly.

Ginnie knew that in such straits her gentle sister's crossness consisted of gazing reproachfully at the offender while tears filled her deep blue eyes. These tactics had successfully repulsed two or three would-be beaux in Cheltenham. Now Lydia was stepdaughter to an earl and, however besotted, the respectable son of the respectable squire was not at all likely to take advantage of her.

Any more than Lord Amis was likely to take advantage of herself, Ginnie thought with a sigh. That kiss had been a momentary caprice, prompted not by admiration but by one of those inexplicable impulses gentlemen were prone to.

Today of all days she did not mean to repine. She went down to breakfast with a spring in her step.

Although Burnham Beeches was no more than a couple of miles from Lord Wooburn's estate, as the crow flies, Ginnie had never been there. The carriages stopped in a clearing of bracken and heather, scattered with graceful silver birches, surrounded by the beech woods. She was fascinated by the ancient trees, so different from the usual tall, slender beeches. Centuries of pollarding had created massive, contorted trunks, easily climbed, as the twins proved ninety seconds after alighting from the carriage.

"I want to climb, too," cried Nathaniel as Colin lifted him down from the gig.

Lady Wooburn, watching Jack and Jimmy with alarm, was moved to protest, "Oh, no, darling, you are too little."

"I'll get him up there safely, Mama," said Colin, "and back down again. Just wait till I tie up Patch, Nat."

The earl soothed her. "Don't worry your pretty head, my love. Trees and boys were made for each other." He exchanged a grin of complicity with Colin and led his wife away. "Come and sit in the shade and I shall tell you about the larch I used to climb when I was a lad. Tall and straight, it was, with branches regular as steps in a ladder, and the top swayed in the wind."

Priscilla went with them. Ten or a dozen other children were halfway up trees, racing with squeals through crunchy piles of dead beech leaves or sliding down the steep sides of a nearby dell. Judith gazed at them wistfully.

"Ginnie, do I have to be a lady today?"

"Certainly not," said Lord Amis's voice behind them.

For once Ginnie agreed with him. "Not today, love. Let me help you kilt up your skirts. If you will excuse us, gentlemen?" she said over her shoulder, leading Judith behind a nearby tree.

"Come on, Justin," said Gilbert. "We mustn't embarrass the ladies."

As she helped her sister tuck her hem into the waistband of her pantalettes, Ginnie wondered if she could possibly have misheard. Had Gilbert really called the viscount *Justin?*

Judith ran off to join the tree climbers. Ginnie paused to greet the vicar and Mrs. Desborough, who drove up at that moment. They presented their son, Mark, who had just arrived home to stay a few weeks

between taking orders and going to be a curate in
Dorset. A tall, fair, willowy young man, he regarded
her with patent admiration and gallantly offered her
his arm.

With his parents, they went over to where Mrs.
Frobisher's servants had spread rugs and cushions on
the thick carpet of last year's fallen leaves.

Ginnie thoroughly enjoyed the picnic. Mark Desborough was flatteringly attentive, even after he had
caught sight of Lydia's lovely face between the two
youthful gentlemen competing with Peter Mason for
her notice. She knew and liked most of the merry
company. The food was superb.

The children, Websters and others, dashed up pe-
riodically to grab a bite to eat, then dashed off again
to play. Colin brought a grubby, happy Nathaniel to
Ginnie, but Alice appeared at once to relieve her of
him and took him off to ply him with goodies. Priscilla sat primly by her mama, who absent-mindedly
fed her on titbits from her own plate.

Though Priscilla seemed perfectly contented, Ginnie asked her, "Do you not want to go with the other
children, love? They are having such fun."

"I don't want to get my frock dirty," she said.

Ginnie smiled and shook her head and turned back
to her conversation with Mark Desborough and Sir
Mortimer Rill.

Talking, listening, or eating, she was constantly
aware of Lord Amis's whereabouts. He moved from
group to group, chatting to everyone with the self-
assurance of the heir to an earldom, yet without the
least sign of condescension towards his less-exalted
neighbours.

He was quite the handsomest gentleman present, especially when he smiled or laughed. Ginnie, who had seldom seen him do either, felt her heart twist within her. Gilbert had called him Justin. Was reconciliation possible at last? Would he one day smile at her, laugh at something she said?

Yet so recently he had put the worst possible construction on her encounter with the odious Sir William and had tried to do her an ill turn with his father. She didn't know what to think.

The eldest of the Masons' daughters, a young woman married to a Beaconsfield lawyer, came up and invited her to go for a stroll. Ginnie glanced about. No sign of the twins. Judith, Nathaniel, and Alice were tossing armfuls of leaves at each other nearby. Lydia was already strolling off with Peter Mason, safely chaperoned by his youngest sister and the two persistent gentlemen. Priscilla was helping herself to a cheesecake, obviously enjoying the change from plain nursery fare.

Justin had settled beside the vicar and was earnestly discussing some weighty subject. His serious, intent expression was as unfamiliar to Ginnie as his smile. He had never looked at her without scorn, or anger, or arrogant complacency, except . . .

Except just before he'd kissed her, when his gaze had devoured her and thrilled her to the marrow of her bones.

"You are wool-gathering, Miss Webster! Do let us take a little gentle exercise."

"I beg your pardon. Yes, that will be delightful."

"Allow me to give you each an arm to lean on, ladies," offered Mark Desborough hopefully.

Accepting, they headed for a path through the trees. Just before the picnic site was hidden by a turn in the path, Ginnie glanced back. Nothing was changed. Greedy little Priscilla was even reaching for another cheesecake.

They wandered about the woods for twenty minutes or so before turning back. By then Ginnie had no notion which of the maze of paths led back to the picnic, though the others, familiar with the place since childhood, knew the way. She hoped, a little anxiously, that the twins had obeyed her injunction not to go too far afield.

In no time they were once more in sight of the rest of the party. With relief, Ginnie saw the twins thirstily drinking lemonade.

As she looked around for the others, Justin sprang to his feet, strode across the intervening rugs, and seized Priscilla. Tucking her under one arm, he ran towards the nearest trees.

"Oh Lord!" Ginnie groaned, and picking up her skirts, she followed at a most unladylike pace.

The glimpse she had caught of her sister's green-tinged face prepared her for what she found behind the huge old tree. Priscilla was bent double, casting up her accounts. Justin held her by the waist, supporting her forehead with one hand, his pained gaze fixed on some distant spot.

"*Thank you,* sir!" Ginnie took over, murmuring soothing words. Priscilla's forehead was cold and sweaty.

With a sigh of relief, Justin stepped back. "Every time I looked up, she was taking a bite of something or other," he explained in a conversational tone. "At first I assumed it was always the same something, but when she stopped eating and started to grow pale, I kept a close watch. Then she clutched her stomach and I decided it was time to intervene. I could not think Mrs. Frobisher would appreciate—''

''Thank you, my lord, you need say no more! Have you by any chance a handkerchief?''

The heaving had stopped and Priscilla was sobbing weakly. Without another word, Justin held out his handkerchief. Taking it, Ginnie was cleaning her sister's face as best she could when Alice arrived.

''Oh, miss, I'm that sorry. Can I help?''

''Yes, bring me a napkin soaked in water, if you please.''

''And a glass of water,'' Justin suggested.

The nursemaid sped off. When she returned, Ginnie asked her to go and keep an eye on Nathaniel and the twins. Priscilla was already feeling a little better. Intent on wiping her face and helping her wash out her mouth, Ginnie was startled when Justin spoke.

''It seems to me Miss Priscilla would be better off at home. May I offer my services to take her back to Wooburn?''

''Oh, I thought you had gone!''

''I want to stay with you, Ginnie,'' Priscilla wailed, clinging to her.

''Naturally my offer extends to both of you.''

''It might be as well,'' Ginnie admitted, regarding her sister's still-pallid cheeks.

''Then if you will go directly to the carriages,'' he said, pointing, ''I shall go and inform our hostess and your mama of our departure and meet you at the curricle.''

"Very well, sir. Pray make my apologies to Mrs. Frobisher. But will you tell Gilbert or Colin or Lydia, not Mama? She will only worry."

"As you wish, ma'am." He bowed slightly and they parted.

"He frightened me when he grabbed me like that," Priscilla confided, hanging on Ginnie's arm.

"I expect he did, but he was actually most helpful, for a wonder. No doubt the spectacle of a member of his family behaving so disgracefully would have humiliated him beyond bearing. It was very naughty of you to eat so much as to make yourself sick."

"I'll never ever eat cheesecakes again. It was horrid and my tummy still hurts. I'm glad Lord Amis is going to take us home."

"Yes, I'd not have expected such kindness of him. I dare say he'd not entrust his cattle to his groom, but he might have told Colin to drive us in the gig."

They reached the clearing where several grooms had charge of the carriages and the mounts of those who had ridden. Some of the more skittish horses were being walked about, including two of Justin's new greys, led by the groom he had hired to take care of his precious, high-spirited team.

Justin arrived just as the man saw her and came towards her. The pair were hitched up to the curricle with their fellows. Justin looked appraisingly at the head-tossing, impatient horses and turned to Ginnie.

"I believe it would be a mistake to have your sister sitting beside me," he said sardonically. "I could not answer for my control of my cattle with the distraction of anticipating a recurrence of her...er...unfortunate illness."

"I shall sit between you," she replied with dignity, hoping that Priscilla would have the sense to lean over the side if she felt suddenly sick.

He handed her up and lifted Priscilla up beside her. Going round the back of the curricle, he took the reins from the groom, who jumped up behind. Then Justin took his seat at Ginnie's side and they set off.

The seat was wider than that of the gig, but not by much. Ginnie found herself pressed against Justin, hip to hip and thigh to thigh. When she tried to shift imperceptibly, Priscilla complained that she was being squeezed half to death. In view of her condition, Ginnie didn't dare increase her discomfort.

As they trotted through the narrow lanes, she tried to concentrate on the flowers in the hedgerows. It was impossible. She tried to ignore the contact with Justin. Equally impossible. His hard-muscled leg tensed and relaxed against her with the sway of the well-sprung curricle. Heat diffused throughout her body, burning in her cheeks and in the pit of her stomach. Clasping her hands tightly in her lap, she bowed her head, praying her bonnet hid her face from him.

And then they came to a sharp corner. In directing the horses, his arm brushed against her breast. The glow within her flared into flame and she gasped aloud.

"Are you all right?" His voice was strained. Risking a peep, Ginnie saw that his gaze was firmly fixed on the ears of his leaders. Then he said in a more normal tone, "Is that wretched child in dire straits? Shall I stop?"

"I'm better," said Priscilla. "I like your carriage, my lord. It's much nicer than riding in the gig with old Patch pulling it."

He made some response and they continued to talk. Ginnie scarce understood a word they said. Though Priscilla's voice had extinguished the flame, the flexing pressure of Justin's thigh continued, and with it the glowing warmth that was slowly but surely melting her.

Just when she was certain she could stand it no longer, the curricle turned between the tall wrought-iron gates of the park. The greys cantered swiftly up the avenue of elms and halted before the front door. The groom sprang down and went to the horses' heads.

Justin lifted Priscilla down and offered Ginnie his hand. Face averted, she reached for it as she stepped down, missed, and stumbled. He caught her against him. For a moment, his strong arms supported her.

Instantly she pulled away. "Thank you, my lord," she muttered. "I must take Priscilla to Nurse." And seizing her sister's hand, she fled into the house in an agony of embarrassment.

"WILL YOU BE GOING back to the picnic, my lord?"

"What?" Justin tore his gaze from Ginnie's rapidly retreating figure. "Oh, no. Take them round to the stables, if you please."

Slowly following her into the house, he wished he had told the groom to walk home from Burnham Beeches, or to cadge a ride on his father's carriage. Ginnie had been grateful for his help. It might have been a good time to attempt to settle his differences with her.

Perhaps not, though, with Priscilla listening to every word. In fact, it had been Priscilla who talked, while Ginnie said not a word from the moment he sat down beside her. Had she recalled her grievances and decided she had nothing to say to him fit to be uttered before a servant? Or had she been as disturbed by his proximity as he had been by hers?

The feel of her taut body against his, the faint fragrance of jasmine, had been far more distracting than Priscilla's presence next to him could possibly have been. In fact, it was just as well that the child and the groom had been with them. Otherwise he might have been tempted to drive Ginnie off to some hidden dell in the woods and ravish her.

This time, he could not possibly blame her for enticing him. He had insisted on her sitting beside him. The only question was, what had silenced her: his touch or the affronts he had so freely lavished upon her?

The need to talk to her, to come to an understanding, was urgent within him as he entered the house. He was making for the stairs to seek her out when Reynolds came into the hall, silver salver in hand.

"There are some letters for you, my lord, and a periodical." The butler went to the hall table, picked up several items and placed them on his tray, then presented it to Justin.

Justin scooped them up, intending to read them after his hoped-for interview with Ginnie. As he went up the stairs, he flipped through them. *The Gentleman's Magazine,* a letter from the Foreign Office, one from

George Medford, one from his aunt, and another directed in an unfamiliar feminine hand.

As he crossed the landing, he broke the seal of the last. Unfolding it, he glanced at the signature: Amabel Fellowes.

Amabel! He had almost forgotten that wretched houseparty. One foot on the bottom step of the next flight, he paused to read her brief letter. Writing on behalf of her parents—a young lady simply did not correspond with an unrelated gentleman—she accepted his kind invitation. She and her mother would arrive in ten days' time, her father two or three days later, as he had business in Town.

He had arranged the house party solely to humiliate the Websters. What maggot had got into his head? Now he had ten days' grace to persuade them he was their friend before his fashionable guests arrived to pour scorn on their artless ways.

# CHAPTER TWELVE

URGENCY GNAWED at Justin. He started up the stairs towards the nurseries at a run. He must speak to Ginnie at once.

Before he was halfway up, he slowed to a halt. Amabel was coming to Wooburn in the expectation of receiving an offer of marriage. She was the perfect bride for him, the daughter of an earl, beautiful, sophisticated, accomplished—everything he could ask for. She had even waited faithfully for his return from Russia, though the understanding between them had been of the most informal kind.

He was going to marry Amabel, so his attraction to Ginnie must be sternly suppressed. He had best not see her now, while the sweet provocation of her closeness lingered fresh in his mind.

With a groan, he changed direction and went to his dressing-room. The door was ajar. He pushed it open as he entered.

A horrendous clatter ensued as a dozen tin pie pans descended upon his unsuspecting head.

One of them clipped him painfully on the ear in passing, though his thick hair protected him from the rest. His eyes watering, he kicked them aside and crossed to his dressing-table, on which he dropped his letters. He peered at his ear in the looking-glass.

It was bright red, though not actually cut. Irresistibly reminded that Ginnie was not the only Webster he had yet to win over, Justin sank onto a chair to think.

The pie pans were the twins' doing, he guessed. They must have heard him giving Tebbutt the day off, and sneaked in before leaving for the picnic. If they had already collected the pie pans, it wouldn't have taken more than a moment to set up the trap. The only contact he had had with Jack and Jimmy was as the butt of their tricks. They were a self-sufficient pair, always together and doubtless egging each other on.

He hadn't the faintest notion how to tackle them. What of the others?

When he started to count, he was pleased to realize he was already on reasonably easy terms with four of them: Gilbert, Judith, Priscilla, and Nathaniel. Setting aside Ginnie and the twins for the moment, that left Lydia and Colin.

Lydia he didn't consider to be a problem. She was as compliant and easygoing as her mother, though she had shown an unexpected flash of spirit in defending Lady Wooburn against his wild accusations. In retrospect, he failed to see how he could ever have believed that gentle peagoose to be a conscienceless schemer.

No sense in repining! The countess had forgiven him—if she had understood his words in the first place—and Lydia would follow suit.

Colin was the best target for the present. His first goal was to learn more about the lad. Since Colin spent most of his time with Mills, Justin decided to seek out the bailiff, whom he also needed to see on his own account. He still hadn't made arrangements with the man to learn about the business of the estate that one day would be his.

On his way to the door, he flattened a pie pan underfoot. With a sigh, he foresaw that the twins would be a stumbling block. He stacked the pie pans and deposited them on his dressing table for Tebbutt to deal with. He'd be damned if he'd go down to the kitchens himself to present them to Cook.

Mills was not in his office, but Duffy knew which direction he had ridden in, so Justin had Prince Rurik saddled and rode after him. He found him leaning on a five-barred gate, discussing with a tenant farmer whether the wheat in that field, known as Bragg's Bottom, was ready to be harvested. They raised their hats to him.

Signalling to the men to continue, Justin listened to their words. Very much aware of his own ignorance, he watched as they each rubbed a picked ear between callused palms, chewed on a kernel or two, and knowledgeably eyed the cloudless sky. The pale gold hillside, splashed with blue cornflowers and scarlet poppies, shimmered in the afternoon heat haze, then rippled in a sudden cooling breeze.

"Best try to get it in afore the weather changes," Mills advised at last. "But don't push 'em too hard, Jake." He pocketed a couple of ears. The men nodded to each other, then the tenant bade Justin goodday and trudged off.

Mills mounted his dun cob. "Thunderstorm within the week," he said laconically. "What can I do for you, my lord?"

A straightforward question about Colin's character would seem deuced peculiar, Justin realized. "Ex-

plain about that corn,'' he requested, hooking a
thumb back over his shoulder as they turned their
horses' heads towards the home farm. ''Why should
it not be ripe when you are harvesting elsewhere?''

''North-facing slope wi' the wooded hill to the west
keeping the afternoon sun off the valley bottom. He'll
get a good enough crop this year, such weather as
we've had, but Bragg's Bottom's best left to pasture,
if you ask me.''

''I saw you put some ears in your pocket.''

''To show Master Colin. He knows what wheat's
like when it's good and ready. This lot'd profit from
another week o' sun but it can't be guaranteed.'' He
grinned suddenly, his teeth white in his lined, weath-
ered face. ''Time to teach the lad the art o' compro-
mise.''

''An important lesson,'' Justin agreed ruefully. To
a diplomat it was perhaps the most useful art of all,
but one he had forgotten when he first met the Websters. ''When I asked you the other day whether Colin
was capable of handling the gig, you gave me the impression that you have a high opinion of him?''

''Aye, my lord, that I do. He's willing, and quick to
learn, and good wi' the men—not just to give orders,
mind, but concerned for their welfare. For his age,
he's a responsible lad. He don't care for keeping the
books, but 'tis not my favourite occupation neither.''

''I cannot blame either of you.'' He thought of
Ginnie faithfully checking Mrs. Peaskot's accounts. ''I
suppose I shall have to learn to understand an account book.''

'' 'Tis important, my lord, as Master Colin under-
stands. The most important thing is, he has a real feel

for the land, a love for it, you might say." The bailiff looked embarrassed at this flight of fancy.

"Does he, indeed!" Justin was not sure he wanted Colin to love the land—his father's land, one day *his* land.

"Aye," Mills confirmed. "I don't expect to have any doubts about handing over to Master Colin in a few years time, and so I mean to tell his lordship."

Justin stared at him. "You are training him to replace you when you retire?"

The bailiff stared back, his bushy grey eyebrows raised in surprise. "Aye, my lord. What else would I be doing?"

"With my father's knowledge?"

"To be sure. You don't think I'd do such a thing wi'out the earl's permission, I trust!"

"No, no, of course not," Justin hastened to soothe the man's ruffled sensibilities. "Whose idea was it?"

" 'Twas young Colin first asked me, but something he said made me think his sister put the notion into his head."

"That would not surprise me in the least."

"You don't object, my lord? In the natural way o' things, 'twill be you he's working for sooner or later."

"No, I don't object, though after a few years of your training, I dare say he will be able to obtain a position anywhere in the country without difficulty, should he choose to."

Mollified, Mills nodded his appreciation of the compliment. They turned to a discussion of what Justin ought to learn about the estate. He didn't need to know the details of ripening grain or pasture versus cropland, but he must be able to take an intelligent interest in his bailiff's work and in the welfare of labourers and tenants.

"So you will have a second pupil," Justin said as the house came in sight, "as soon as my guests have left Wooburn."

"Aye, my lord. I'll be setting up for a schoolmaster next. You'd do well, though, to have a few words wi' the squire as well. There's no better landowner hereabouts, for all he's always got a joke on the tip o' his tongue."

"I shall. In the meantime, I'll ride out with you and Colin now and then."

"You do that, my lord." The man's eyes twinkled, crinkling at the corners as if he were enjoying some secret joke.

Mills turned off on a farm track and Justin rode on towards the house. So Ginnie had suggested that Colin learn estate management, preparing the lad to earn a living, he thought. How could he have been so mistaken about her character? Everything he learned about her now that his eyes were opened made him admire her more: her loving care of her brothers and sisters; her insistence on not taking advantage of his father's benevolence; her practicality, including the skilful supervision that had made his home such a pleasant place to live.

Pleasant, that is, except for the tricks that had been played on him. He had deserved them, he acknowledged ruefully. He had rushed in like a terrier into a rat-infested barn. Having once given credence to what the scandalmongers were saying, he had refused to believe the evidence of his own eyes.

His lips tightened in a flash of anger at Amabel's eagerness to repeat the gossip. Yet he could not hold her greatly to blame; she was only following the example of the ton. Once she was his wife, he'd make it plain that he did not care for such tattle.

Approaching the house, he saw his father's carriage returning from the picnic and went to meet it. Before he reached it, it stopped before the front door and the twins tumbled out, a pair of dishevelled ragamuffins. One saw him and nudged the other. Two freckled faces glowered at him. They turned their backs with deliberate rudeness and scampered towards the lake.

"Master Jimmy, Master Jack, come here this instant!" The new nurserymaid, Alice, had descended from the carriage, burdened with a drowsy Nathaniel.

"Let me take him," Justin offered, swinging down from Prince Rurik's back and tossing his reins to the footman who jumped down from the back of the carriage. "You'll have enough on your hands with the twins."

"Thank you, my lord." The girl passed the child to him, picked up her skirts, and ran after the boys.

As the earl handed Judith and his countess down from the carriage, Nathaniel sleepily put his arms around Justin's neck and laid his weary little head on his shoulder. Justin's heart swelled with unexpected emotion. He had always assumed that one day he would have an heir, and probably other children, but the notion had been abstract. Now, the prospect filled him with a sudden delight.

*His* children would be well brought up and properly disciplined, he resolved as Alice returned towards the house with a firm grip on each of two grubby collars.

All the same, on the whole it was amazing how well the young Websters had turned out, considering their mother's indulgent, far-from-authoritative nature. Had Ginnie been entirely responsible for her siblings' upbringing? For the first time he was curious about their father, about their past.

Carrying Nathaniel into the house, he promised himself a long and serious conversation with Virginia Webster in the near future.

GINNIE DREADED her next meeting with Justin. As often as she told herself he could not possibly have guessed the strange, delightful yet terrifying sensations that had nearly overwhelmed her, she was determined to avoid him.

That evening she did not go down to dinner. The sultry weather had given her the headache, she claimed. Despite her guilt at Mama's and Lydia's dismayed solicitude—she was *never* ill!—she did not waver. The very thought of being near Justin made her tingle all over.

Sooner or later she'd have to see him, but time, she hoped, would lessen his alarming effect on her.

Lydia came up to her chamber after dinner to ask how she felt. "Step-papa wished to send for the doctor," she said. "I told him you would not like such a fuss made and Justin persuaded him to wait until the morning, unless you should feel worse tonight. Justin said this hot, close weather is enough to give anyone a megrim and likely a fuss would only make it worse. He said Mr. Mills expects we shall soon have a storm, which will cool the air.''

"I hope he is right.''

"But thunder is so horrid! Ginnie, I believe Justin cannot be quite so horrid as he sometimes seems. Tonight he was truly concerned for your comfort, I am sure. He is quite in Mama's favour now, and Gilbert and Judith like him, and Priscilla.''

"He was amazingly kind to Pris today,'' Ginnie conceded. Yet she could not forget overhearing his attempt to deprive Gilbert of an education, herself and Lydia of a chance to find husbands. He had her emotions in a whirl. "I don't know what to think,'' she said despairingly.

"Don't try to think while your head aches, dearest,'' Lydia said soothingly. "Only, will you mind very much if I do not sew up any more of his clothes? So that he cannot put them on, I mean.''

"No, of course not, Lyddie. You have far too much sewing to do already. I don't know what we should all do without your hard work and your clever needle.''

"Mama does a great deal of sewing, too,'' she said, but she looked pleased by the praise.

Ginnie wondered with another wave of guilt whether she neglected Lydia because she was so placid, never causing any trouble, never demanding attention. She dearly loved her eldest sister and best friend. How she'd miss her when she married! Perhaps Lyddie would accept Peter Mason's hand after all, rather than that of some London gentleman, and thus remain in the neighbourhood of her family.

If so, Ginnie would not lose her company, for she had every expectation of staying at Wooburn Court herself, taking care of her brothers and sisters until she dwindled into an old maid.

Suddenly the prospect was unbearable. One day Justin was bound to marry and bring his bride to Wooburn. How could she endure that?

Her invented headache was rapidly becoming real.

That night her dreams were confused. She woke feeling restless and rose early to go down to breakfast while Justin was taking his usual morning ride. Then, for the first time, she took advantage of the arrival of Miss Tullycombe, Nurse, and Alice to go for a walk in the park on her own.

The air was still and oppressive, already losing its morning coolness under the assault of a brassy sun. Though the lake reflected a cloudless sky, somewhere beyond the horizon, thunder rumbled, faint in the distance. Despite the heat, Ginnie shivered. She did not care for thunderstorms, though for years she had pretended not to mind them for the children's sake.

After hurrying down from the house, she paused in the shade of a willow to catch her breath. From the shelter of its drooping branches, she saw Justin cantering homeward, a straight, proud figure on the superb bay stallion. Her thoughts flew back to their first meeting. How much of his enmity was due to the humiliation of being thrown by Prince Rurik, practically at her feet? Would they otherwise have been friends by now? Wistfully, she watched him ride on before she continued along the path to the beech wood.

It was cooler in the wood and the thunder was inaudible. With an effort, Ginnie put Justin out of her mind, determined not to let the wretched man spoil her enjoyment of the freedom of walking at her own brisk pace.

SEVERAL LETTERS awaited Justin at the breakfast table. Over his usual solitary meal, he broke seal after seal to find pleased acceptances of his invitations.

The Parringales—why the devil had he invited them to Wooburn? He did not even like the couple. Her tongue was as malicious as Sally Jersey's, a byword in a milieu not given to sparing the victims of gossip. As for her husband, Ferdie, though merely the younger son of a baron, he could trace his family tree back to the Norman Conquest, and he never let anyone forget it.

The Honourable Alfred Bascom was a harmless enough fop whose mind never rose above his clothes. Nor did his sister's. Lady Pierce aspired to lead fashion, succeeding only in following it to extremes, whereas Lord Pierce was a dandy after the fashion of Beau Brummel, eschewing all extremes. Like Brummel, he prided himself on his wit, frequently sharpened at the expense of his wife's excesses.

Justin brightened as he opened the third letter. Thank heaven George was coming, though he might turn tail when he discovered the identity of his fellow guests. His little sister, Lizzie, was indeed on the brink of making her come-out. A house party at Wooburn sounded like the ideal occasion to let her dip her toes in the waters of social intercourse.

He was looking forward to making the aquaintance
of Lord Wooburn's new family, George wrote. Justin
was suddenly glad that he had merely mentioned their
existence to his friend, not poured out on paper the
furious condemnation he had felt at the time.

The fourth letter was from his aunt, Lady Matilda
Hardwick, his father's only sister, enclosing notes to
the earl and his wife. She had been in Brussels with her
soldier husband, had gone on to Paris after Waterloo, and had only just, quite by chance, heard of her
brother's remarriage. A sensible, good-natured
woman, she was preparing to dash home to lend her
countenance to her new sister-in-law. Whatever
dreadful mistake poor Egbert had made in choosing a
bride, she said, a breach in the family was what she
would not stand for.

Knowing his aunt, Justin grinned. If his will to
continue the feud with the Websters had not already
withered, Lady Matilda's arrival would have blighted
it in short order.

The letters gave him an excuse to seek out Ginnie,
to discuss provisions for the comfort of the visitors.
His grin faded as he wondered how he was to account
to her for his peculiar choice of guests. And ought he
to warn her that he had invited Amabel to Wooburn
with the firm intention of requesting her hand in
marriage?

# CHAPTER THIRTEEN

IN SEARCH OF Ginnie, Justin went first to the morning-room. The small room was hot and airless though the windows were wide open, the curtains half-drawn against a flood of sunshine. There he found Lydia, her golden head as usual bent over her needle.

Raising her vivid blue eyes from her work, she smiled, a breathtaking sight. She really was the loveliest creature, yet her face lacked the character and animation to be found in Ginnie's less-perfect features.

Justin returned her smile. "Good morning, Miss Lydia. I must have a word with your sister. Do you happen to know where she is?"

"Ginnie went for a walk, sir. I do not know in which direction."

"Alone?"

"She will not go beyond the park, but she likes to be alone sometimes. She has not often had the chance."

"I suppose not," Justin agreed, reflecting on how much he enjoyed his solitary morning rides. "And you, you don't mind being alone? You prefer your embroidery to walking with her?"

"It is not embroidery. I seldom have time for embroidery. This is a shirt for Colin." She spread the white cambric to show him. "Large as he is, he keeps growing. The boys always need shirts."

"You make them all?" he asked, taken aback.

"Oh yes. Ginnie says it would not do for a countess to be found sewing shirts or mending. Mama does any sewing that will not shock ladies who call on her."

"Good Lord, this will never do. Is there no sewing woman in the house?"

"Ginnie did hire a woman from the village to mend the household linen when first we came to Wooburn Court," said Lydia guiltily. "It had been dreadfully neglected. Mama and I simply could not manage it and keep the family decently dressed as well."

"Of course you could not. My dear Lydia, I am not finding fault with you in the slightest."

"You cannot blame Ginnie!"

With a bewildered feeling that the conversation was escaping him, Justin said firmly, "No one is to blame. I shall see that a seamstress is hired as soon as possible, as a permanent member of the staff. And an abigail," he added with reckless abandon.

"But Mama has an abigail," Lydia protested. "Ginnie said—"

"—That a countess must have a personal maid," he guessed, completing her sentence. "But so should you and Ginnie. Will she condemn my shocking extravagance if I insist on your hiring at least one lady's maid between the two of you?"

Her blank look made it all too plain that she did not understand his teasing. Justin left her to puzzle it out for herself, took his leave, and went out to the stables. Riding about, he was bound sooner or later to come across either Ginnie or Mills and Colin.

He was trotting uphill on a flinty track between stubbled fields when the steward rode his Welsh cob over the brow of the hill towards him. Behind Mills towered a huge Suffolk Punch, with Colin perched on its back like a small child on a fat pony.

"What the devil!" Justin drew rein and stared, torn between surprise and amusement.

Colin's sun-browned face flushed as the chestnut cart-horse stopped beside Mills. "Good day, my lord," he echoed the bailiff with evident reluctance.

Though half the Suffolk's bulk, Prince Rurik was not much shorter, but he stood downhill. Justin craned his neck backwards and said with a grin, "Does it give you delusions of grandeur?"

Colin's flush deepened. "At least Daisy is reliable and good-natured," he retorted.

"I advised the lad to ask his lordship for a proper mount," said Mills, his eyes bright with mirth. So this was his secret joke!

"I wager Miss Webster forbade it." Justin was as certain as if he had heard the words.

"Yes, she did," said Colin defiantly.

"Well, I seem to be contradicting a great many of your sister's prohibitions these days, so we'll look about for something more suited to your size and dignity."

"You mean you'll buy me a horse?" The boy looked both eager and incredulous.

"I shall. The Wooburn stables are sadly depleted these days."

"Could you..." Colin started, acutely embarrassed. "Would it be possible... You see, I'm on the large side, but I don't mind looking a bit of a fool if you'd only buy a smallish horse, so that Gil and the girls could ride sometimes.''

Mills nodded approval, as if his favourable opinion of his protégé had been borne out.

"Your sisters ride?" Justin asked.

"They used to, before my father sold the manor. Just ponies, of course—even Ginnie wasn't quite grown up then.''

"Ponies," said Justin thoughtfully, tucking away in his mind the information about the late Mr. Webster. "The twins ought to be learning to ride. Mills, keep your ears open for a couple of children's ponies, will you?''

"Aye, my lord."

"They had best be as near identical as possible, to avoid squabbles. That may take some time. Colin, not a word to your brothers. I don't want to raise their hopes too soon. Meanwhile, you and I shall seek out mounts for yourself and Gilbert and the ladies.''

"For all of us?" he gasped.

Justin smiled and shrugged his shoulders. "There's plenty of room in the stables," he said.

"And plenty of likely lads wishful to be taken on as grooms," said Mills.

"Send 'em to Duffy," Justin told him. "Where are you bound? I'll go with you."

They rode on together, talking of estate business. Impressed by Colin's grasp of matters of which he himself knew nothing, Justin was glad he had made the effort to become better acquainted with the lad.

They had stopped to speak to a score of women and children gleaning in a harvested field when a scrawny boy of ten or twelve pushed through a gap in the hedge. The group parted as he ran up to the bailiff. Anguish, excitement, and fatigue fought for ascendency on his scratched, tear-besmirched face.

"Mr. Mills, please, sir, me da's hurt bad. Near cut his leg off wi' his scythe. Mam says will you come, please, sir. I bin looking for you all over."

"Bragg's Bottom?" asked Mills curtly.

"They carried him home, sir."

"Has the doctor been sent for, Davy? No? Colin, off wi' you to Beaconsfield for the doctor."

"I'll go," said Justin, already turning Prince Rurik's head. "It will be quicker. You'd best come up behind me, Davy, to direct the doctor."

As a kerchiefed woman lifted the boy onto the stallion's croup, Mills nodded in acknowledgement. "Aye, my lord, but I'd be glad if you'd come straight back and have a word wi' Jake Robinson. Accidents will happen, to be sure, but he pushes his men too hard."

"He do be a hard master, m'lord," another of the gleaners volunteered.

"I'll speak to him while the shock is upon him," Justin promised. "I'll not have my father's tenants mistreating their hands. Hold on tight, lad."

As he urged his mount to a trot, he thought he heard, through a murmur of approval from the gleaners, Mill's laconic voice saying, "He'll do."

"He's a great gun," came Colin's enthusiastic reply.

A warm surge of pleasure brought a smile to Justin's face. Prince Rurik sailed over the hedge and galloped on with his double burden.

Luckily, they found the doctor at home. He took the boy up in his gig and Justin cantered back cross-country towards Robinson's farm. Storm clouds were massing overhead; an occasional gust of wind raised a swirl of dust from the dry ground. In the pastures cattle huddled in uneasy groups, but in the arable fields reapers and gleaners worked with an urgent intensity. Justin realized that Jake Robinson had been racing to get his crop in before the fine weather broke, yet the farmer could not be permitted to endanger his labourers.

When he reached the wattle-and-daub cottage that was Davy's home, Robinson was just emerging, his expression belligerent. Justin called to him and dismounted, tying Prince Rurik beside Daisy and Mills's Welsh cob. The farmer came over, hat in hand, his pugnacity changing to a look of harassment. He stood staring at the ground while Justin made it plain to him that if he wished to renew his lease come Michaelmas, he must have more care for the welfare of his people.

"And I suggest that in future you take Mr. Mills's advice on the best use of a piece of land," he finished, recalling the steward's opinion that Bragg's Bottom should be left to pasture. He dismissed the sullen man and turned to the cottage.

"Well said." Ginnie stood on the doorstep, smiling at him. Beneath her chipstraw hat, her face was pink, her ringlets limp. The hem of her lilac walking dress was liberally coated with dust. She looked hot and weary and bedraggled.

"What are you doing here?" he enquired, concerned.

Her smile faded. "I know it is Mama's duty to visit the tenants, but she—"

"I meant no criticism," he said hastily. "It is admirable that you should respond so quickly to their need."

The grey-blue eyes searched his, saw his sincerity. "I brought a basket of provisions. The family has lost its breadwinner and will be in sore straits. Temporarily, one must hope, but he is badly cut and has lost a great deal of blood. Is the doctor coming?"

"Yes, but he'd have been here sooner had they sent for him at once."

"He would not come without Mr. Mills's authority, I collect, for fear of not receiving his fee."

Justin frowned, dismayed. "That will not do. I shall assure him that in future he may count on me to pay for any services to my father's dependents."

"You must not blame your father," Ginnie said gently, guessing his thoughts. "He has not had the heart to take an interest in his estate since . . . since he lost your mother."

"But *your* mother has restored his *joie de vivre*," he said with a wry smile. "I—"

A rumble of thunder interrupted him. A flurry of raindrops spattered down and they retreated into the cottage.

The dimly lit ground floor of the tiny dwelling was a single room, crowded now. On a wooden settle by the fireplace lay a man in a blue smock. Mills and Colin bent over him, struggling to bind a fresh cloth over the bloodstained rag that wrapped his calf. A woman stood nearby, her anxious gaze fixed on her injured husband, a babe in her arms and toddlers clinging to her shabby, neatly patched skirts.

"Her eldest daughter is a dairymaid," Ginnie said quietly. "She will be required at home now, yet they need her small wages."

"I'll make up the money. Do you think I should offer the lad, Davy, a place as stable-boy?"

"An excellent notion. Tell her, and relieve her mind of a part of her troubles." She nudged him towards the woman.

He went to speak to her, and was relieved when the doctor arrived in a crash of thunder to end her tearful gratitude. Colin and Mills made way for the physician's ministrations. A moment later two neighbour women came in, shawls thrown over their heads, doubtless driven from the fields by the rain that now pelted down from the leaden skies. They hesitated on the threshold, awed by the exalted company within.

"Time we were off," grunted Mills.

"You can't walk home in this, Ginnie," Colin pointed out. "You'd best come up with me on Daisy. You'll only be drenched instead of drowned."

"On Daisy!" Ginnie's alarm made the men grin. "But she's so very... large."

"She's very gentle and she can carry two easily."

"So can Prince Rurik," Justin said, intervening, "and he will get you home sooner. Wait here a moment while I bring him to the door."

Ignoring her obvious uncertainty, he dashed out, before realizing that haste was futile. By the time he had untied Prince Rurik, who whickered a nervous greeting, his shirt was sticking clammily to his back. He mounted and rode over to the cottage door.

Colin helped his sister up. She perched uncomfortably on Prince Rurik's withers in front of Justin, her hat rapidly disintegrating under a torrent from the thatched eaves.

"Hang on to his mane with one hand," Justin ordered, "and lean back."

She obeyed, holding herself stiffly. He put one arm about her slender waist and gave Prince Rurik the office to start. There was no hint of romance or passion in his clasp—he was simply glad of the spot of warmth against his chest as the heavens clashed above and the rain poured relentlessly down.

Ginnie's clothes were soaked through within moments. She scarcely noticed the fact, nor Justin's arm steadying her. Out in the open, the storm was much more terrifying than she had dreamt possible. Clutching the stallion's mane, she willed herself not to curl up in a ball with her hands over her ears and her eyes shut tight.

She half succeeded. The flare of lightning penetrated her closed eyelids; crack after crack of thunder deafened her. Fright and the damp chill combined to produce a spasm of shivering.

Justin's clasp tightened. His nearness was a strong, unyielding refuge, a shield against the raging elements. Beneath her she felt Prince Rurik's solid vigour, the regular drumming of his hooves combating the tempest's chaos. Gradually she relaxed and let her two protectors guard her from harm.

Justin guessed her unreasoning fear, knew the moment when she allowed herself to trust him. For years her family had relied upon her to shelter them from the world. Now, for a brief space of time, she relied upon him. A tender protectiveness rose in him.

Through the storm they galloped homeward.

# CHAPTER FOURTEEN

"I MUST SPEAK to you," said Justin urgently, following Ginnie into the house.

"Yes, but not just now!" Meeting a footman in the hall, Ginnie caught a glimpse of the man's startled expression before he put on his stolid mask. She was suddenly aware of her appearance.

The dust on her hem had turned to streaks of mud. The thin muslin of her gown and shift clung soddenly to her skin. Her hair hung in dripping draggle-tails about her neck, and the brim of her hat sagged over her ears.

"Not now!" she wailed, and sped towards the stairs.

"A hot bath for Miss Webster at once, John," Justin ordered behind her, his voice filled with amusement, "and a fire in her chamber."

At least, after he had seen her in such a disgraceful state, he'd never again be tempted to take liberties with her person. She tried to persuade herself she was glad of that.

A bath and her sister's soothing ministrations soon restored her equanimity. Lydia brushed her wet hair as they sat by the fire, a welcome luxury even in August, for rain still streamed down the window-panes though the thunder had receded to an occasional distant rumble.

Ginnie told Lydia about Justin's handsome behaviour at the labourer's cottage. "He will be a good landlord, I believe," she said, "however difficult he is as a relation by marriage."

"I am not perfectly sure," said Lydia, her smooth brow creased in perplexity, "but I think he said he meant to hire a dressmaker and an abigail for us."

"Heavens, what has come over him? He told me he wishes to speak to me. I assumed he was merely going to discuss arrangements for his guests, as Reynolds mentioned that he received several letters this morning. Can he possibly intend to call a halt to hostilities?"

"Only Jimmy and Jack still dislike him. Even though they have only morning lessons during the summer, they hate having a governess, and they blame Justin for hiring Miss Tullycombe."

"Step-papa did say it was Justin's notion. Oh dear, I have never thanked him, and whatever the twins' opinion, her presence is a blessing. I must go and find him."

"Your hair is just dry enough to put in curl-papers."

"Drat curl-papers," said Ginnie. "Ringlets take too long. Braid it and pin it up, Lyddie, there's a dear."

"It is still damp. You will catch cold."

"I'll wear a cap. Go and borrow one of Mama's."

Lydia returned with a delightful confection of lace and jonquil ribbons. Examining her reflection in the glass, Ginnie wrinkled her nose. In itself quite becoming, the cap made her look like an old maid.

Before she could decide whether to risk taking a chill, there came a knock at the door. It was Tebbutt.

"Lord Amis's compliments, miss, and he'll be in the library for the next hour, if you would find it convenient to join him."

Forgetting the cap, Ginnie refused Lydia's offer to go with her and made her way down to the library.

Despite her rejection of Lydia's support, she was quite relieved to see Gilbert hunched over his books at one end of the room. A branch of candles stood on the table beside him, but the rest of the library was dimly lit by grey daylight. Absorbed in his studies, her brother failed to notice her entrance. Justin, however, turned from the window where he had been gazing out at the rain and came eagerly towards her.

"Ginnie—Miss Webster..." he began in a low voice, with a glance at Gilbert.

"Ginnie," she said softly, offering her hand, "if we are to cry friends."

"I hope so." He took her hand in a warm, disturbing clasp and led her back towards the window. As she sat down on the window-seat, he exclaimed, "Good Lord, why on earth are you wearing that frightful cap?"

"It's a very pretty cap."

"Very fetching, to be sure." He looked down at her, devastatingly handsome with a smile tilting the corners of his firm mouth, a glint in his dark eyes. "But unless you have aged several years in the last hour, you ought not to be putting on a spinster's cap. In fact, I cannot imagine why you were not wed long since."

"I trust I am not yet at my last prayers!" said Ginnie, indignation stilling the flutter in her breast.

"Precisely what I have just said. You have an admirer in Mr. Mark Desborough, I believe . . ."

"He called this morning—to enquire after Priscilla's health."

". . . And I don't doubt there have been other beaux."

"Beaux who failed to become suitors when they realized that I was not only penniless but encumbered by a large family I could not possibly abandon."

"Yes, your family." He sat down beside her, running his fingers through his hair. Ginnie edged back into the corner to increase the few inches between them. Ruefully he asked, "I could not have misinterpreted the situation more completely, could I? Can you find it in your heart to forgive me?"

His closeness was not the only cause for embarrassment. She studied her tightly clasped hands. "If we are to talk of forgiveness, I must needs beg yours, too. I could have stopped the children, but I positively encouraged them to make you uncomfortable."

"Short of actual injury, I have it on good authority—Nathaniel's."

"And Mama's marrying your father in the first place was my doing."

"So you informed me. It has been forcibly borne in upon me that you acted for the best. Come, let us cry quits and start anew."

"They *are* happy, are they not? Your papa was so sad and lonely. . . ."

"It was his notion that I should join the diplomatic service," Justin said defensively.

"He told us. He was very proud of you, going off to do your part against Boney."

"As his only son, I did not feel it right to become a soldier."

"Very proper. Nonetheless, he was lonely. I could tell the moment I first set eyes on him."

"How did you meet?"

"You know that the earl went to Cheltenham to take the waters? No, I dare say he would not tell you. He was very pulled about after a bad attack of the influenza in the spring. One wet and windy Sunday in April we were coming out of church when Mama's umbrella blew inside out. Lord Wooburn offered his, in the most gentlemanly manner, as his carriage was waiting for him. Mama would have sent Colin to return the umbrella to him, but I made her go herself."

"Having discovered who he was, and that he was a widower," said Justin drily.

Ginnie flushed. "Well, of course. We were all to pieces, though we had moved to the cheapest lodgings I could find. I was quite in despair."

"The fact is, for all your mama's amiability, and much as she loves her children, it was you who maintained the family, you who took charge."

Her flush deepened. "Yes," she said simply. What a managing female he must think her! She tried to explain. "You see, Mama is too trusting and too diffident—"

"Too feather-headed," he corrected her, looking sardonic.

"She is not precisely clever," she agreed, "and when Papa died she was with child. And Gilbert was very young, only twelve."

"You must have been all of fifteen."

"Sixteen. Quite old enough to run a household."

"Positively matronly. Your father's death left you in straitened circumstances?"

"We were purse-pinched for some years before that, but Papa was always optimistic, always certain his next scheme was bound to restore the family fortunes. He even hoped to be able one day to buy back the manor." Her eyes filled with tears as she remembered her handsome, cheerful father.

Justin thrust a handkerchief into her hand. "You did not always live in lodgings in Cheltenham, I collect," he said with unexpected sympathy.

"Oh, no." Having surreptitiously dried her eyes, Ginnie proudly raised her chin. "Papa was a country gentleman, a Herefordshire squire, and Mama's father was a baronet."

"It should have been perfectly obvious to me from the start that you were all gently bred. I was determined to be blind, I suppose."

"Hush! We are agreed to let bygones be bygones, are we not? I have been meaning to thank you for employing Nurse and Miss Tullycombe and Alice. They make my life very much easier."

"I am glad of it. I hope the provision of a seamstress and an abigail will ease Lydia's life."

"So she did understand you correctly! It is very kind in you, but we scarcely need an abigail."

"You will when the seamstress has refurbished your wardrobes. It must reflect upon my father and on me if you go about in shabby dress."

"Shabby! Lord Amis, frugal is the word."

He laughed. "Frugal, if you will—and my name is Justin. Frugal or shabby, you would not put me to shame before my guests? I believe we had best supplement the yet-to-be-found seamstress's efforts with a visit to some local dressmaker. Will you find out who is best, and soon?''

"Oh yes, Mrs. Frobisher will know." Ginnie's heart sang at the prospect of pretty gowns after years of making do.

"You must have riding habits. With my father's permission, I shall be purchasing several horses."

"Horses! Justin, you cannot be serious. Can Steppapa really afford so many frivolous expenses?"

"He has spent little for years, and I am not one to outrun the constable." He paused with an arrested air. "Doubtless I shall have to learn to understand our man of business's accounts as well as Mills's. Mrs. Peaskot has a high opinion of your ability in that regard. Will you help me?"

"Of course, if I can, though household accounts are surely simpler."

"I feel certain you will prove equal to more complicated bookkeeping methods."

"I only wish I were certain I am equal to providing for your house party. I have never done anything like it before, and Mrs. Peaskot has not for many years. Have all your guests accepted?"

"Yes, though Lord Trenton will join us a day or two later than the rest. Also, I'm afraid my aunt has announced that she is about to arrive from Paris."

"I know!" Ginnie groaned. "I mean, Mama showed me the kindest letter from Lady Matilda and I shall be delighted to make her acquaintance, but I wish she were not coming at the same time as everyone else. Will you describe the guests to me so that I know what to expect, how best to make them comfortable?''

To her surprise, Justin looked ill at ease. She recalled her suspicion that he had not intended meeting his friends to be a pleasant experience for the Websters. Surely now that they were reconciled, his changed attitude to her family would determine that of his friends.

''You will like Aunt Matilda,'' he said hurriedly. ''She is forthright and strong-willed, even somewhat dictatorial at times, but tolerant and friendly. She is determined to offer your mother her support.''

''Then I like her already. Lord Hardwick will not come with her?''

''Not this time. He is a lieutenant general with the Army of Occupation in Paris.''

''Who else is coming? I did not bring the list you gave me.''

''There's George Medford and his sister, Lady Elizabeth Innes. I was at Eton and Balliol with George.''

''He is a marquis, is he not?'' Ginnie asked a trifle nervously.

''Yes, but not in the least high in the instep. He's the best of good fellows. Lizzie I remember as a tongue-tied schoolroom miss. She's of an age with Lydia, about to make her bow to Society. I hope they will be friends.''

''If not, it won't be Lydia's fault.'' She prayed that Lady Elizabeth was pretty enough not to resent her sister's looks.

"Then there is Bascom. He was at Eton with George and me. You must promise me you will not laugh when you see him."

"Laugh? Why should I?"

"Alfred wears the highest collars, the widest, stiffest cravats, the gaudiest waistcoats, the largest gilt buttons, the most padded shoulders, the tightest... shall I go on?" he enquired as Ginnie raised her hand to her mouth too late to stifle a giggle.

"I believe I have the picture."

"Worse," Justin said gloomily, "his dress is his only subject of conversation, and his sister is much the same. When ruffles are à la mode, Lady Pierce has more ruffles than anyone else. When hemlines rise, hers rise farthest. When transparent muslins are worn, hers are practically invisible."

"Good heavens, I cannot wait to see them. What of Lord Pierce?"

"You have heard of George Brummell, the Beau?"

"Yes, who has not?"

"Pierce is a counterfeit Brummel, a would-be witty, fastidious dandy who despises his wife's taste."

"Oh dear," said Ginnie, the only response that came to mind. Mr. Bascom and the Pierces did not sound congenial.

"At that," Justin continued, "Pierce's feeble wit is to be preferred to the tedious pomposity of Parringale's conversation, if conversation is the word for it. As for Mrs. Parringale, she is known to the ton as Parrot Parringale because she constantly echoes the words of others. Every scandalous, hurtful on-dit is guaranteed dissemination by her tongue."

Ginnie was startled by the dislike in his voice. "But they are your friends!" she protested.

"Acquaintances," he said shortly, his face closed. "Excuse me, pray. I must go and consult Mills about that unfortunate family."

Hurt and angry, she realized that he had deliberately invited people he did not care for simply because he knew they would hold her family in contempt—and show it.

He had not described Lord and Lady Trenton and their daughter, Lady Amabel Fellowes. Was the omission because they were even less agreeable than the rest, or because they were true, intimate friends? Somehow Ginnie found the possibility that Lady Amabel might be Justin's intimate friend quite unbearable.

All in all, she began to dread the house party.

FULL OF REMORSE, Justin strode down the passage to Mills's office. He had intended only to warn Ginnie, to put her on her guard against the detestable people he had been bacon-brained enough to invite into his home. Instead he had vexed and distressed her.

She was too shrewd not to have guessed his purpose in issuing the invitations. He ought to have stayed to assure her that he regretted his damnable folly, but he had escaped to avoid speaking to her of Amabel.

"About as much pluck as a dunghill cock!" he jeered at himself. Ginnie surely was aware that he was bound to marry, if only for the sake of an heir, and whom he wed made no difference to her. Sooner or later she would learn that the daughter of the Earl of Trenton was his chosen bride. Given the expectations he had raised, he was in honour bound to offer for Amabel, like it or not.

And he *did* like it, of course, he affirmed hastily. His equal in birth and fortune, handsome and accomplished, with a preference for him, tried and proven during his long absence—what more could he demand in a wife?

With a strong sense of relief, he reached the steward's room and entered. In discussing with Mills a plan to ensure the prompt services of the doctor when needed, he shut out the memory of Ginnie's reproachful gaze.

By the time Justin went up to change for dinner, the rain had stopped and a brisk wind was rapidly sweeping the clouds from the sky. He began to hope that the wind of common sense would clear the clouds from Ginnie's brow, reminding her that invitations once sent could not be recalled, however much he might prefer to do so.

He wished he had waited a few days to strengthen their fragile friendship before he warned her of his guests' less-agreeable characteristics. The renewed breach between them was surprisingly painful. Until she accepted his change of heart, his peace accord with her family was incomplete.

He stepped into his dressing-room. Tebbutt stood there staring at the dressing-table with a revolted expression on his face.

"The rain must've brought 'em out," he said.

"Brought what...oh Lord!" He surveyed the heap of snails with disgust. Several of the boldest were exploring their surroundings, leaving slimy trails across his toilet articles and the mirror. "The rain may have brought them out, but it didn't bring them in," he observed grimly.

"Still, could've been worse. They could've put 'em in your bed."

Justin shuddered. "Give them to Miss Judith for her hedgehog. I'll wager those devilish twins are to blame." He'd forgotten that not only Ginnie remained to be won over.

# CHAPTER FIFTEEN

WHEN JUSTIN EMERGED from his dressing-room, Ginnie was lurking on the landing, waiting for him.

"I know you cannot rescind your invitations now," she assured him earnestly. "Never fear, Justin, we shall somehow contrive to satisfy your guests."

Grateful for her magnanimity, Justin smiled at her. His heart was oddly light as they went down the stairs together. No, nothing odd about it: he had succeeded in turning a family of enemies into friends—most of them, at least.

His guests should have nothing to sneer at in their dress, he vowed, regarding Ginnie's unadorned pink cambric gown with disfavour. Tomorrow he'd set about acquiring new wardrobes for every one of them, even the wretched twins.

He was glad he had sworn Judith to secrecy about the snails. She had been pleased to be saved the trouble of hunting them in the garden for her creatures, but he didn't want Ginnie upset by her brothers' misbehaviour. With any luck, new clothes would pacify Jack and Jimmy, and if not, ponies surely must. Justin resolved to remind Mills to treat the acquiring of a pair of ponies as a matter of urgency.

Dinner was a family occasion, none of the neighbours having ventured out after the storm. At ease with everyone at the table for the first time, Justin thoroughly enjoyed the meal. Everyone was merry, as if the end of his quarrel with Ginnie had lifted a damper from their spirits.

He noted Lady Wooburn's care in selecting the best bits of every dish to tempt her husband's erratic appetite, and how the earl ate every bite on his plate to please her. Far from being the disaster he had imagined, the marriage had proved exactly what his father needed. As Lord Wooburn surreptitiously patted his wife's hand, Justin caught Ginnie's eye and they exchanged a glance of perfect understanding.

He was going to enjoy having a large family, and he couldn't wait to see Ginnie—and Lydia, of course—dressed in stylish new gowns.

THREE DAYS LATER, the first new clothes arrived. Ginnie was in the schoolroom, listening to Priscilla reading a fairy tale aloud, when Alice came in with an armful of parcels.

"These here's for the children, miss. Miss Lydia says will you come at once to try on your gowns."

Ginnie hurried down to Lydia's bedroom, already carpeted with a tangle of string, brown paper, and tissue paper. In no time they were gazing at each other in admiration.

Lydia's morning gown of white jaconet muslin flared from the high waist to a hem flounced with rows of French work alternating with narrow rouleaux of mull. Knots of satin ribbon in her favourite deep blue added a touch of colour. The skirt swayed charmingly as she moved. Her happy smile delighted Ginnie.

"Nothing could make you prettier, Lyddie dear, but how prodigious smart you are!"

"So are you, Ginnie. Is it not pleasant not to be dowdy any more?"

"Very pleasant." She looked down with satisfaction at her own walking dress. Of pale green muslin sprigged with darker green leaves, it boasted three wide, dark green frills edged with blond lace around the skirt. The high waist was bound with a green satin ribbon with long ends that fluttered behind. More lace trimmed the bodice and sleeves, and a triple fall of lace adorned the throat. "We need not blush to meet Justin's fashionable friends."

"It is excessively kind in Step-papa and Justin to buy us such lovely things. *All* of us. It must have cost a great deal. I wish I could do something to thank them."

"Now that you have time on your hands, why do you not embroider a pair of slippers for Step-papa and net a purse for Justin?"

"The very thing!" Lydia clapped her hands. "I shall start right away."

"Will you not go for a stroll with me? It is a glorious afternoon."

Lydia shook her head. "I cannot. Mr. Peter Mason said he meant to call this afternoon. With his sister, of course. I have just time to go and see that the children's new clothes all fit them properly."

"When I was up there, the twins had already gone out. I must remember to tell them that on no account should they play in the mud or climb trees in their new clothes." Ginnie picked up her new parasol, white with green ruffles. A lutestring spencer and a glorious bonnet completed the ensemble, but she decided regretfully that a short stroll in the park on a fine day did not call for such splendour. "Mama is out, so in case we have other callers to be entertained, I'll just walk around the lake," she said.

Justin had persuaded Gilbert to go with him to fish in the lake. Not that she was in any hurry to display her finery to Lord Amis—she merely wanted to thank him for his generosity.

The earl's money had paid for the clothes, but the earl himself had never noticed his stepchildren's shabbiness. The moving force was Justin. When he revised his opinion of the Websters, he had done so thoroughly. Ginnie was quite prepared to believe that his churlishness had been the momentary aberration of a normally equable and benevolent nature.

Now they could settle down to a pleasant, peaceful friendship. Since she no longer had reason to be angry with him, his presence would soon cease to agitate her.

Approaching the lake, she eagerly scanned the banks. There was no sign of the anglers. Disappointed, she strolled on along the path until she reached the point where it divided. A broad ride led into the beech wood from which Justin had galloped to their first, hostile meeting. A narrow footpath continued along the bank, thickly grown here with willow and alder.

She paused to furl her parasol. Unnecessary in the shade of the trees, it might catch on a low bough and tear.

"Gilbert!"

Her sedate, studious brother was perched in a willow, rod in hand. The trunk leaned out over the water, part of it nearly horizontal, and a thick branch paralleled it, not a foot above the water's still surface. Gilbert sat on the trunk, his muddy booted feet on the branch.

"Hush, you'll frighten the fish."

Ginnie lowered her voice. "That's the twins' favourite spot for fishing for minnows. Is there anything larger?"

"Justin says it's quite a deep pool and he's caught perch here. He's gone a bit farther along. Careful, don't come any closer. There's a quagmire under those leaves."

She hastily jumped back, lifting her hem. "Your new evening coat and pantaloons have come."

"No hurry, I'll try 'em on later. Oh, is that a new gown?" he enquired belatedly. "Most dashing. Now do go away, Ginnie. Something might bite."

Pleased to see him interested in an outdoor occupation that took him away from his books for a while, Ginnie went on. Intentional or not, that was another blessing to thank Justin for.

She found him standing under an alder, intent on the cork float bobbing at the end of his line. He had taken off his hat, coat, and cravat. The close-fitting buff waistcoat over his snow-white shirt was moulded to every taut muscle of his back. Dappled sunlight played on his light brown hair as he raised his rod slightly and stepped forward. Ginnie held her breath.

"Lost it, devil take it!" He began to reel in his line.

"Was it a big one?"

He turned his head, startled, then grinned. "The one that gets away is always a whopper. I beg your pardon for my language; I was not aware of your presence."

"I did not want to distract you, nor to frighten the fish, having already been reprimanded by my brother for speaking too loudly. It was an excellent notion to introduce Gilbert to angling."

"I thought he ought to get out in the fresh air more often, and it may take some time to find him a suitable mount." Leaning his rod against the tree, he came towards her. "Ah, I see one of your new gowns has arrived already. Charming!"

He spoke lightly, but the frank admiration in his eyes brought heat to Ginnie's cheeks. "I don't know how to thank you. Lydia is in raptures. She has never complained about the lack, but she does love pretty things."

"And you?"

"Indeed, I am more than delighted. We have so much reason to be grateful to you, I scarcely know where to begin."

"I am trying to make up for a slow start. For going backwards from the starting post, in fact. It is the least I can do for my new family."

He put his arm round her shoulders in a brotherly hug. His touch made her quiver. She gazed up at his suddenly intent face and he slowly raised his hand and traced her parted lips with one gentle fingertip, his arm tightening about her.

His hand moved to the curve of her hip, caressing, pressing her to him. And then his mouth was on hers. As his tongue invaded her mouth, a sharp sweetness

invaded her loins, a hollow, aching need for she knew
not what. She clung to him, strengthless, her being
concentrated in the throbbing spot where his hard
virility met her feminine softness.

"Ginnie," he groaned. "Ginnie, you tempt . . .
ouch!"

Clapping his hand to the back of his neck, he swung
round with a wild glare. From a nearby hazel bush
came muffled sounds of glee. He stalked towards it.

Two small, grubby figures erupted from the bush
and fled. Justin lengthened his stride, reached out,
grasped two collars, and shook the twins as a terrier
shakes a rat. A popgun fell to the ground between
them.

At that moment, Ginnie would not have protested
had he strung her brothers up from the nearest tree.
Her face burning with humiliation, she picked up her
skirts and ran.

By the time she reached the house, slipped in by a
side door, and scurried breathlessly up to her room,
she was having second thoughts. The twins had saved
her from ruin. Another moment of Justin's passionate embrace, and he could have had his way with her
with nary a protest from her lips. Possibly he had been
sufficiently in command of himself to stop before it
was too late—but she didn't think so.

"Temptress," he had started to call her. Did he
blame her for their mutual lapse from propriety?
Once, his opinion had had little power to hurt her.
Now tears pricked her eyelids at the thought that he
might consider her a trollop. She wanted his respect
and friendship more than anything else in the world.

More than anything else except his love.

But the words he had murmured were of tempta-
tion, not love. He desired her body, not her heart. Was
his heart not his own to give? Had Lady Amabel already taken possession?

Racked by jealousy, Ginnie sat on the edge of her
bed and buried her face in her hands.

JUSTIN GLOWERED down at the two dirty, scared,
freckled faces. "Don't you dare to breathe a word of
this to a soul," he said between clenched teeth, "or
you will regret it for the rest of your short lives."

One of the brats shook his head; the other nodded,
wide-eyed. Letting go of their collars, Justin stooped
to retrieve the popgun. He recognized it. They must
have found it in a toy chest in the nurseries.

When he straightened, they had already vanished
among the trees. He could only hope he had put the
fear of death into them.

What a devil of a coil! He dared not punish Jack
and Jimmy beyond the confiscation of their toy gun.
If they felt they had nothing more to lose, they might
talk, not understanding that he would suffer less than
their sister from the resulting scandal.

She was irresistible, he thought, as, with unsteady
hands, he tied a rough knot in his neckcloth and
donned his coat. She set his blood on fire, tempting
him beyond bearing. Yet this time he had no inclina-
tion to blame her for enticing him into that inexcus-
able and unforgettable embrace. The fault was all his.
He wanted her. If only he were free . . . but he was as
good as promised to Amabel.

He must marry Amabel as soon as possible. Once
he had a legitimate outlet for his baser urges, he'd

cease to feel this aching desire for Ginnie. He'd be able to enjoy her friendship, to admire her many excellent qualities without reservation.

Fishing had lost its allure. He needed some more active pastime to distract him. He picked up his rod and was turning to leave when he saw Ginnie's new parasol lying abandoned on the ground.

With a tender smile he was unaware of, he stooped to retrieve it. She deserved to be indulged with every frippery her heart might desire. She had praised her sister for uncomplaining patience, but it was her own active refusal to accept a life of hardship for her family that had raised them from indigence.

Brushing the leaf-mould from her parasol, he vowed that henceforth her life should be as easy as he could make it.

EVERY TIME GINNIE was sure her list was complete, she or Mrs. Peaskot thought of something else that needed doing before the guests arrived. She was glad to be busy. She simply had no time to go into a decline from unrequited love.

The weather continued fine and Justin was out a good deal, riding with Colin and Mr. Mills or consulting local landowners about his estate duties. Though he had curtailed his early morning rides in favour of joining her and Gilbert, Colin, and Lydia for breakfast, she saw little of him. They were scrupulously polite to each other.

For a couple of days, Ginnie managed to avoid the twins altogether. She knew she ought to reprimand them for shooting Justin with the popgun, but she quailed at the prospect. It would be better for everyone concerned if that particular incident were quietly forgotten.

Then three days before the house party, quite by chance, she caught them sneaking along the passage towards Justin's bedchamber.

Jimmy had a bulging, squirming, squeaking sack over his shoulder. Jack was playing lookout, but his brother's agitated burden drew his attention for a moment. He jumped a mile when Ginnie crept up behind him and tapped him on the shoulder.

"What . . . ? Oh, it's just you, Ginnie. You startled me," he said reproachfully.

"I meant to. What on earth do you two think you are doing?"

"It's the stable cat." Jimmy returned to join them.

*"Miaaaow,"* wailed the sack, confirming his words.

"It's going to have kittens."

"Any minute."

"The stables are dirty."

"And draughty."

"And the horses might step on them."

"Or the grooms."

"We reckoned they'd be more comf'table in Justin's bed."

Eyes sparkling, they appeared to expect plaudits for their charitable concern for the cat's welfare.

*"Miiaaaow!"* came the muffled, desolate cry again.

"If she or the kittens have come to any harm, Judith will dip you in boiling oil. Take her back to the stables at once! And then I want a word with you in my chamber."

Abashed—but not very—they departed.

Ginnie continued to her bedchamber, where a superb gown awaited her. It had been created especially for the Masons' summer ball, to which both family and guests at Wooburn Court were invited. She spared it a perfunctory glance and then began to pace, wondering how she might persuade the twins to abandon the feud with Justin.

If only she knew whether they considered themselves to have rescued her from his unwanted attentions. She suspected that her presence had been incidental, that he had been their target long before she came on the scene. Impossible to ask, impossible even to mention that occasion!

They arrived. With expressions of saintly innocence they stood before her, hands behind their backs.

"It's all right."

"Judith put it in a basket."

"With an old blanket."

"It's already started having kittens."

"But they would have been *very* comf'table in Justin's bed."

"He would not, however!" she exclaimed. "You really must stop harassing him."

"Just because all the rest of you have given in," said Jimmy scornfully.

"It's like the fable."

"The lion and the oxen."

"From Aesop. United we stand," Jack proclaimed.

"Divided we fall."

"Just because he's started giving you things."

"You've forgotten what a villain he is. He called you dreadful names."

"And he made Mama cry."

"But, boys, he has seen the error of his ways. He knows he was mistaken in believing us to be wicked. He is doing his best to make up."

"He's humbugged you."

"He can't bamboozle us. He hired Tully just to bother us."

"And then he made us have fancy clothes we can't have any fun in."

"We'll show him."

"We're not so easily gulled."

Ginnie utterly failed to convince them that Justin's intentions were now of the best. If only Duffy were not having such trouble finding suitable ponies! In the end she resorted to forbidding them to play tricks on Justin. "Promise," she insisted.

"We promise."

"We won't play tricks on *him*."

They exchanged a glance of complicity. What were they up to now?

"And if you spoil his house party, Mama and I shall be held more to blame than he will."

"He invited them."

"Tully says we have to stay out of their way," said Jack resentfully. "They won't want children running around."

Before Ginnie could extract another promise, Lydia came in to see her gown, and Jack and Jimmy escaped.

The glory of lilac crape over white satin with a van-dyke bodice had Lydia in raptures but failed to relieve Ginnie's anxiety. Even if she made the twins swear to behave, she was afraid they would invent some ingenious justification—such as the comfort of a pregnant cat—for doing precisely as they chose.

Justin might have some ideas as to how to thwart them. At least she owed it to him to warn him that she feared her brothers still intended mischief.

# CHAPTER SIXTEEN

As THE DATE of the house party approached, Justin found himself in a state of unaccustomed trepidation. Having chosen his guests deliberately to discomfit the Websters, he faced with misgivings the possibility that they might actually do so.

At last the Websters were all dressed as befitted their new station in life, and they had naturally good manners that raised not an eyebrow amongst their country neighbours. By the finicky standards of the Beau Monde they might at worst be judged provincial. Only the most captious of critics could find faults worthy of comment, but Justin had to admit he had invited several people who took pride in seeking out the most insignificant of faults and gossiping about them. They were quite capable of holding his step-family up to ridicule.

On the other hand, he thought as he changed for dinner that evening, he had learned that the Websters were not easily cowed. They had collectively snapped their fingers at his condemnation. The high-nosed contempt of a party of strangers was unlikely to overset them.

The trouble was that Lady Amabel was destined not to remain a stranger.

That thought so disturbed him that he realized he had reached the true source of his uneasiness. He was in a quake at the prospect of proposing to Amabel.

And that was ridiculous. In London, not six weeks since, he had viewed the task with equanimity, as the necessary prelude to the acquisition of a suitable wife. He knew himself acceptable to her father in birth and fortune, to herself in character and person. The only possible reason for her refusal might be his sudden acquisition of nine younger siblings. At the very least, they were an added responsibility she'd have every excuse not to relish. Was that the source of his anxiety?

Whether or not that was the whole truth, after leading Amabel and her parents to expect a proposal, he had no choice but to offer for her hand. Yet, should she reject him, the humiliation would be devastating, an irreparable blow to his pride.

Torn by conflicting emotions, Justin went down to the drawing room. As he entered, he had a sudden sense of history repeating itself. No one was there yet but Ginnie. At the open French windows, she stood gazing across the terrace at the twilit gardens. The last rays of the setting sun gilded her ringlets. Hearing his arrival, she turned.

"I'm glad you have come down early, Justin." She stepped towards him. "I must speak to you."

Remembering, he moved to place a chair between them, leaning with folded arms on its high back. She was an enchanting sight in a new gown of leaf green sarcenet, flounced and frilled in the latest mode, yet no more delectable than she had been that first day. From the very beginning she had unsettled him, destroyed his vaunted composure, wrecked his peace of mind.

"What can I do for you?" he asked coolly.

"I don't know. I simply don't know what to do. I don't even know if I am making a mountain out of a molehill."

Now that she was closer, he saw that she was worried. "Tell me," he said more gently. "Perhaps I can relieve your apprehensions, and if not, I shall give you any help I can. Is it something to do with my guests?"

"Yes, in a way. It's Jimmy and Jack. I have a lowering feeling that they are plotting to disrupt the house party."

"They are your brother's and your responsibility," he snapped. Nothing would more surely shame him before Amabel and the others than the sort of tricks the twins conceived. He could not expect a gently bred, fastidious female to overlook their antics. "If they dare to cause trouble, if they dare distress Lady Amabel, I shall take a strap to them," he vowed.

"No! You shall not!" Despite her own exasperation with the twins, her fear of their disgracing the family, Ginnie flared up in their defence. "They are only mischievous little boys. They don't mean any real harm."

"They must learn that their mischief will not be tolerated."

"I will not let you touch them."

They glared at each other in impotent fury as a footman came in to light the candles. He was followed by the earl and countess, before whom it was equally unthinkable to quarrel. Then Gilbert and Lydia joined them.

"What's the matter?" Gilbert hissed in Ginnie's ear. "I swear you look like the Chimera, with smoke and sparks issuing from your nostrils."

"I'll tell you later," she whispered back.

Brooding over her dinner, she concluded that while she'd never let Jack and Jimmy be beaten, a warning of the likelihood of such a fate might do them good. She might not even have protested Justin's threat had he not mentioned Lady Amabel in the same breath.

Lady Amabel was his only concern, it seemed. The possible distress of his other guests did not appear to vex him in the least. He must be desperately enamoured of her.

Ginnie seethed with jealousy. Lady Amabel was the daughter of an earl, doubtless beautiful, demure, well dowered, and a pattern-card of propriety. In no way could the daughter of an impoverished country gentleman compete. True, Ginnie had won Justin's passionate embrace, but that merely demonstrated his lack of respect for her. He'd never so insult Lady Amabel—before marriage.

He must dread that the twins' misbehaviour would give Lady Amabel a disgust of his family and induce her to reject his suit. Ginnie decided she would be positively grateful if her brothers' capers prevented a betrothal, even if their want of conduct put her to the blush.

On the other hand, if Justin truly loved Lady Amabel, he'd be unhappy without her. Ginnie did not want to see him unhappy. His unhappiness might be even more unbearable than his marriage to Lady Amabel, or, indeed, to anyone other than herself.

Ready to martyr herself for his sake, Ginnie resolved to keep a close eye on the twins and to ask Gilbert, Lydia, and Colin to do likewise.

After dinner she had no opportunity for a private word with Gilbert and Lydia, as the vicar, Mrs. Desborough, and their flatteringly attentive son came to take tea. If only Mark Desborough stirred her pulses as Justin did!

At last they left. She and Lydia retired to her chamber, where Gilbert soon joined them.

"You've come to cuffs with Justin again, haven't you?" he accused her. "What crime has he committed now?"

Lydia protested. "I am sure Justin cannot have done anything very dreadful."

"No, he hasn't," Ginnie conceded reluctantly. She could not explain her pique without telling them about Lady Amabel, which would mean revealing that she loved Justin. "He was thrown into high fidgets because I warned him that Jimmy and Jack are ripe for mischief and may embroil his guests."

"I should rather think he might be!" Gilbert exclaimed. "Only conceive how mortifying for all of us! But it would be worst for you, Ginnie, because you and Mama would be blamed, and Mama is unlikely to notice anything amiss. How frightful to be held up to ridicule by Justin's grand friends!"

"Positively horrid," Lydia agreed, shaken.

And how utterly unendurable to be held up to ridicule by Lady Amabel, Ginnie thought, aghast. "You must help me watch the twins every waking moment," she begged.

For the next three days she scurried around more busily than ever, and nearly drove the servants to Bedlam with her demands. Everything must be quite perfect for Lord Amis's friends. Lady Amabel should find no excuse to despise her housekeeping, at least.

Justin's aunt arrived the day before the other guests. A small, wiry woman, Lady Matilda Hardwick had an imposing manner despite her lack of inches. She arrived in midafternoon, and having quickly summed up the situation to her own satisfaction, sent for Ginnie to come to her dressing-room before dinner.

Ginnie attended her with her head held high, ready to defend herself and her family. If she chose, Lady Matilda could undoubtedly make their lives difficult.

"My dear," she said at once, instantly reassuring Ginnie, "I can see that my poor brother has acquired an admirable family. I congratulate you."

"M-me, my lady?" Ginnie stammered.

"You, and none other. Your mama is a pretty widgeon," she said forthrightly, "a good-natured widgeon, and she suits Egbert surprisingly well, but she has not an ounce of spirit. In fact, she is not at all up to snuff. Hardwick and I shall be back in England by the spring and I've a mind to do the Season. If you wish, I shall sponsor you and your sister."

With more immediate problems weighing on her, Ginnie had scarcely spared a thought for her sister's come-out, but she was properly grateful. Though her fervent thanks owed more to her relief at Lady Matilda's approval than to the offer, her ladyship was pleased.

"I have not been blessed with children," she said, "and being always surrounded by young officers, I have not felt the lack of sons. Yet I always thought I should have liked to have daughters. You may call me Aunt.''

Buoyed by Aunt Matilda's favour, Ginnie looked forward to the house party with considerably diminished anxiety.

THE FOLLOWING DAY, the first to arrive were George Medford and his sister. The Marquis of Medford, far from proving a formidable figure, was a slight, unassuming young man with a charming smile. From the moment he entered the drawing-room, his gaze was fixed on Lydia.

Used to evoking such behaviour in susceptible gentlemen, Lydia paid him no more attention than that required by courtesy. She was occupied in trying to set his sister at ease. Lady Elizabeth, a pretty girl with brown hair and brown, doelike eyes, was desperately shy. Lydia, though her disposition was far from lively, had never suffered from shyness. Taking Lady Elizabeth under her wing, she offered to show her to her chamber, and they went off together.

Justin promptly bore off Lord Medford, promising to return when the next guests arrived.

Ginnie sat down with her mother and Lady Matilda, the earl having cannily sequestered himself with Gilbert and his books.

''Lord Medford seems very pleasant,'' she said hopefully. Perhaps all the guests would turn out equally agreeable.

''Medford is a nice boy,'' Lady Matilda agreed. Like the countess, she had an embroidery frame before her, but while Lady Wooburn had continued to set industrious stitches, Lady Matilda had been too busy watching everyone. "And Lydia is a kind-hearted girl who will soon be on intimate terms with his sister."

Guessing her train of thought, Ginnie said with a smile, "You must not read too much into Lord Medford's stunned expression, Aunt. Few gentlemen set eyes on Lydia for the first time without looking like veritable mooncalves."

"Very likely, my dear, but what a coup it would be to catch her a marquis!"

"You must not look too high. Papa was only a country gentleman."

"My girls are fit to marry the highest in the land," Lady Wooburn said stoutly.

Lady Matilda patted her hand and said, "Of course, Emma dear." Ginnie was amused to note that she had already adopted the soothing manner towards Mama common to her children and her husband.

The next to arrive were the Honourable Alfred Bascom with his sister, Lady Pierce, and her husband. Ginnie did not need Reynolds' announcement to guess their identities, so exactly had Justin described them.

From head to foot, Lady Pierce was dressed *à la militaire*. Her hat was a shako with gold braid and a white cockade. Her Wellington mantle had gold epaulets on the shoulders, and her pelisse *à la hussar* was frogged down the front and liberally braided everywhere else.

"I see my costume makes you stare, Miss Webster," she observed with a dismissive glance at Ginnie's sprig-muslin morning dress. "I dare say you patronize a country seamstress? Military fashions are all the rage in Town this year.''

''M'wife's hoping Bonaparte escapes again,'' her husband drawled sarcastically, ''so that she can rush into battle.'' Lord Pierce wore a superbly fitted dark blue coat over an ivory waistcoat. His neckcloth was of moderate height, tied with simple precision. Dove-coloured inexpressibles, glossy, white-topped boots, and a single fob completed his toilet. Not a hair was out of place.

His brother-in-law looked like a caricature of him. The gilt buttons on Mr. Bascom's wasp-waisted pea-cock coat were as big as saucers. Daffodil waistcoat clashed with primrose pantaloons. Huge gold tassels adorned his boots, half a dozen jewelled fobs dangled at his waist, and his cravat was a miracle of intricacy that appeared to be strangling him. His bow to the ladies was a model of discretion—if he had bowed any lower his shirt-points would certainly have gouged out his eyes.

Ginnie bit her lip to suppress a giggle.

''Fancy you're admiring my cravat, ma'am,'' he said condescendingly. ''Invented the knot myself. I call it the Metropolitan because only those well acquainted with London modes can appreciate its finer points.'' Like his sister, he dismissed Ginnie's new gown with a glance, relegating her to the ranks of those unacquainted with the highest kick of fashion.

''Popinjay,'' Lady Matilda snorted in her ear.

Comparing Mr. Bascom's, and even Lord Pierce's attire with Justin's casual morning dress and Lord Medford's riding clothes, Ginnie agreed and felt better. Lady Elizabeth, too, was much more simply dressed than Lady Pierce, more suitably for the country. Nonetheless, Ginnie was glad of her new wardrobe.

She wondered whether Lady Amabel favoured the extremes of fashion. Surely not, since Justin had spoken slightingly of Lady Pierce's taste. On the other hand, love was said to be blind. Ginnie waited in a fever of impatience for the arrival of Lady Amabel and her mother.

As if to thwart her, the Parringales came next. Mrs. Parringale wore floating draperies of an acid green that reminded Ginnie of her nickname, Parrot, and the colour complemented her acid tongue. Within a few minutes of entering the drawing-room, she was regaling Lady Pierce with a "delicious on-dit" about Wellington and Lady Wedderburn-Webster.

"Right in the middle of the park in Brussels," she exclaimed in her high-pitched voice. "They disappeared into a wooded hollow, without the least discretion. Is it not shocking? And then her mother arrived in a carriage and went snooping after her, without success, I understand. I am speaking of Lady Mountnorris, Miss Webster. No doubt you do not know the people of whom I speak. I dare say you have never met the Duke of Wellington?"

Ginnie was obliged to admit to the lamentable deficiency in her acquaintance. She was next subjected to an interrogation by Mr. Parringale regarding her antecedents. That her father was an untitled country gentleman did not dismay him. However, when he discovered that the Websters could trace their ancestry through no more than three generations, he deserted her in favour of the daughter of a marquis. Too timid to flee, Lady Elizabeth was forced to listen to two centuries' worth of the Parringale family tree before Justin realized her plight and rescued her.

He brought her to Ginnie. "You will be comfortable with Miss Webster," he told her, smiling, but with a hunted look in his eyes. Turning to Ginnie, he said softly, "My apologies. Don't say I didn't warn you."

"The reality vastly surpasses your descriptions," she said wryly, meeting his gaze with understanding and acceptance of his remorse.

"Lady Trenton. Lady Amabel Fellowes," announced Reynolds.

The Countess of Trenton completely obscured her daughter. A massive woman, triple-chinned, encased in a tentlike garment of dull purple, she waddled forward to meet Lady Wooburn. Ginnie thought of a few remarks worthy of Mrs. Parringale that she'd like to address to Justin on the subject of daughters growing to resemble their mothers.

Then she saw Lady Amabel, a striking, willowy figure in flame-coloured lutestring trimmed with black. Beneath a bonnet of flame velvet surmounted by three black plumes, raven ringlets set off a perfectly oval face with a full red mouth and dark, lustrous, black-lashed eyes. Ginnie immediately felt utterly insipid. It was quite impossible to conceive of so glorious a creature ever approaching Lady Trenton's mountainous stature.

Justin had turned as the ladies were announced, so Ginnie had not been able to witness his expression. However, Lady Amabel swept forward, holding out her hands to him, ignoring both her hostess's prior claims and the two young ladies at his side.

"My dear Amis, we are reunited at last," she fluted, confirming Ginnie's every suspicion. "How I have longed to see your home."

Perforce he took her hands and raised one to his lips as he bowed. "Welcome to Wooburn, Lady Amabel. Allow me to present you to my stepmother."

"Ah yes, the rapacious widow," she said, scarcely troubling to lower her voice as she laid a possessive hand on his arm.

Justin winced, knowing that Ginnie must have heard. "The Countess of Wooburn," he admonished, leading Amabel across the room.

"Of course. I most sincerely commiserate with you, Lord Amis, and I pity your poor father."

As he might have guessed, Lady Wooburn failed to understand and therefore to be offended. "Pray do not disturb yourself, Lady Amabel," she said in her soft voice. "Lord Wooburn is not unwell. He has gone off to study his books when he ought to be here to make everyone welcome. I shall scold him, I promise you, but I doubt it will do any good. He is quite the scholar, you know," she added proudly.

"You have done him a world of good in wresting him from his studies to be more sociable." Justin said kindly. It was the first time he had voiced his gratitude. She beamed at him. If Amabel was disconcerted, she did not show it.

His aunt, meanwhile, was regarding him with a minatory eye. All too plainly, she disapproved of his choice of guests. Hastily he introduced Amabel to her.

"Lady Matilda, how I have longed to meet you. I am resolved to be on the friendliest terms with all Lord Amis's relations."

Aunt Matilda gave him a startled look. He hastily turned away to greet Lady Trenton.

"Such a pity Trenton is delayed," that lady boomed. "You will have to possess your soul in patience for another day or two, dear boy."

As he once more escaped, taking Amabel back to meet Ginnie, he heard Lady Trenton continue, "An understanding of long duration, Lady Wooburn. My dear Amabel turned off any number of suitors while..."

He suppressed a groan.

Ginnie, her face pale but her chin defiantly raised, avoided his eyes as she stood to greet Lady Amabel. She did not curtsy, and Justin was proud of her dignified bearing. Beside Amabel's striking flamboyance, she had a simple elegance that he suddenly found infinitely more attractive.

Amabel nodded coolly. Her uninterested gaze passed over the modestly dressed Marquis of Medford, who had come to join his young sister.

"Lady Amabel," said Ginnie, "may I present Lord Medford and Lady Elizabeth Innes."

"Lord Medford!" Amabel instantly decided that George was worthy of her notice after all. She fluttered her long eyelashes at him. "Have we not met before? At Almack's, perhaps?"

"Hardly, ma'am. Being an indifferent dancer, I never attend Almack's. I shall take Lizzie in the spring, of course," he added as his sister looked up at him anxiously.

"You'll be expected to take to the floor at the Masons', George," Justin told him.

"I shall enjoy that. A few country dances with congenial people is quite different from the formal waltzes and quadrilles at Almack's."

"The squire has invited us all to a ball next week," Justin explained to Amabel.

"La, a country hop, how tedious. But I have a famous notion. Why do you not give a ball here at Wooburn, Lord Amis, to celebrate our...to amuse your guests?"

"Perhaps we could." He caught Ginnie's aghast expression. "Just a small, informal affair for our neighbours, if it would not be too much work, Ginnie?"

"No, I expect Mrs. Peaskot and I can manage it," she said valiantly. "We do owe our neighbours some entertainment."

"Local gentry!" Amabel exclaimed in scorn. "My dear Miss Webster, that may do very well for you, but it is not at all what I had in mind, I vow. Even in the country and at short notice, a dress ball given by Lord Amis cannot fail to attract any number of people of consequence."

"However, an evening of dancing for my guests and neighbours is what I have in mind," said Justin firmly. "*If* my father and my step-mama agree. We'll discuss it later, Ginnie. Do you care for a stroll in the gardens, Lady Amabel?" He hustled her out, willy-nilly, before she had a chance to slight anyone else.

If he had still hoped that his guests' polish would show up the Websters as shabby-genteel, he'd have been sorely disappointed. Amabel knew how to behave at a royal drawing-room, and she would never do anything to incur the censure of Almack's patronesses. Yet Ginnie had in her little finger more of the natural good manners that stem from consideration for the feelings of others.

Why had he never before noticed Amabel's lack of courtesy? Of course, he had only seen her surrounded by those whose opinion she valued. Also, he had to admit, he had been dazzled by her striking beauty, her birth and fortune, and her preference for his company.

She was no whit less beautiful now, her birth and fortune remained impressive, and she undoubtedly considered him her future husband. As they turned into the shady yew walk, out of sight of the house, she stopped and raised her face to him, her eyes expectant.

# CHAPTER SEVENTEEN

JUSTIN KISSED AMABEL, and it left him utterly unmoved. He knew he had to marry her and he hoped to reanimate his wish to make her his wife. But he had felt more emotion on shaking George's hand after their long separation. How long ago it seemed, how young he had been, when first Amabel's beauty and vivacity had attracted him.

"I beg your pardon," he said stiffly, moving away from her. "It was unforgivable in me to take advantage of being alone with you."

Her trilling laugh, which had once enchanted him, now made him feel a complete jobbernowl. "My dear Justin, I wonder that you have never kissed me before. After all, we are as good as betrothed. Surely you do not suppose that Papa might refuse his permission when he comes? We might even have been wed by now, I vow, were it not for your own father's *mésalliance* having forced you to rush down here."

"I do not consider my father's marriage a *mésalliance*."

"La, you are all forbearance. To be sure, what is done is done, and you will soon be able to banish the widow and her brood to the dower house, no doubt."

Since only his father's death could bring that about, Justin was appalled by her insensitivity. "Not for many years, I trust," he said, frowning.

His offended tone must have penetrated her self-absorption, for she began to praise the gardens of Wooburn Court. "The country can be quite pleasant in the summer," she observed. "However, one is always glad to escape back to Town in September, I vow."

Justin made no effort to correct her misconception that he intended to spend most of the year in London once they were married. Somehow he was going to persuade her that she did not want to marry him.

For how could he marry Amabel when he loved Ginnie?

As they strolled, as Amabel chattered on, his growing dislike of her had suddenly put his feelings for Ginnie into perspective. Ginnie was everything Amabel was not. She lacked Amabel's birth and fortune. She was pretty, whereas Amabel was beautiful. But she was kind and loving, loyal, steadfast, equally ready to throw her energies into protecting her family or into the practical matters of the household.

Ginnie was warm, and sweet, and altogether desirable. He ached to hold her. Next time he kissed her—and there *would* be a next time, he vowed—he'd do it deliberately and thoroughly, and he'd tell her he loved her.

He dared to hope that she might love him, too. She had not pulled away from his embrace in the woods, had even begun to return his passion when . . .

He started as Amabel demanded his opinion. "Shockingly vulgar, was it not?"

Though he had not been attending, he had a vague idea she had been repeating an on-dit about Princess Charlotte. "I don't care for scandal," he told her abruptly. Her rumour-mongering had caused his feud with the Websters.

She stared at him in surprise. "But everyone gossips," she protested. "People are quite the most amusing subject of conversation."

He did not trouble to explain the difference between innocent gossip and the kind of malicious tittle-tattle that spread false tales, held people up to ridicule, and ruined reputations. He was not going to marry her.

To his relief, they rounded the end of the yew walk to find that several of the others had come out to stroll in the gardens. He and Amabel joined Alfred Bascom and Mrs. Parringale. After a few minutes, he claimed a need to speak to his other guests and slipped away.

Ginnie was not in the gardens. Justin returned to the drawing-room and narrowly avoided being waylaid by his aunt. Lady Matilda, he was sure, had several pungent comments on her lips regarding Amabel's and Lady Trenton's broad hints of forthcoming nuptials.

He managed to avoid her, only to learn from Reynolds that Ginnie, George, Lydia and Lady Elizabeth had gone down to the lake. For the moment he gave up his attempt to see Ginnie. It would be just as well if he had a scheme prepared for repulsing Amabel before he avowed his love for Ginnie. He racked his brains.

By the time he dressed for dinner, no plan had occurred to him beyond the adoption of a discouraging manner. He went down to the drawing-room early to make sure all was in order. Though he did not doubt Mrs. Peaskot's or Reynolds's competence, many years had passed since Wooburn had accommodated guests, and Ginnie had never before entertained a house party.

The drawing-room was pleasantly welcoming, with a vase of tall phlox in the fireplace and sweet peas elsewhere scenting the air. A tray of drinks stood on a table. The evening sun shining through the French windows reminded him of the dust-up he had had with Ginnie over the twins. If she had forgiven him for that, making the acquaintance of his guests had no doubt put her back up again.

He had allowed himself to forget that Ginnie was not always warm and sweetly desirable. When vexed, she was as prickly as Judith's hedgehog. With an indulgent smile, he recognized that before he attempted to persuade her of his love, it was not merely just as well, but rather, imperative to dispose of Amabel's claims upon him.

Crossing to the connecting door, he glanced around the dining-room. White linen, gleaming silver, and sparkling glass met his eyes. On the table and the sideboard, Reynolds had already set out several cold dishes under silver covers. Justin went over to peek under the largest. A galantine of veal, decorated with slices of lemon and sprigs of parsley and mint, whetted his appetite. Cook had obviously put forth her best efforts.

He returned to the drawing-room and was about to close the door behind him when a sound made him turn. The door to the dining-room from the hall was opening, very, very slowly.

Justin promptly closed his door all but a crack and applied his eye to that crack. He was not at all surprised to see a segment of freckled face topped with ruffled blond hair inch round the other door. A blue eye scanned the room.

"*Psst,* all clear." Jack—or perhaps it was Jimmy—disappeared. "Hurry up."

For the first time he had caught the wretches in the act. And he had absolutely no urge to stop them.

At worst, they would annoy his guests. At best—or rather, at *their* worst—they might succeed in convincing Amabel that she wanted nothing more to do with Wooburn Court and its inhabitants, including him.

He watched, fascinated, as a twin advanced furtively into the dining-room bearing in both hands, with the greatest care, a dish with a silver cover. Making his way to the sideboard, he stared in dismay, then turned his head.

"Jimmy," he called in a piercing whisper, "there's no room here!"

Jimmy darted in to join him and hurriedly rearranged the dishes already set out. "Put it there. *Quick.*"

Once again a sound behind Justin made him turn. The door from drawing-room to hall was opening.

Quickly and quietly he closed the connecting door as Ginnie came in. She was wearing a gown of a smoky blue grey lavishly trimmed with white lace, but she could have been in rags for all he cared.

"You look beautiful," he said, moving towards her.

"It is a pretty dress, is it not?" she said distractedly. At any other time the compliment would have delighted her, but Lady Amabel was about to come down and enjoy finding fault with her arrangements. How could Justin have fallen in love with such a spiteful, supercilious female?

She gazed about the room. To her it seemed both elegant and comfortable. It was smarter than the Rills' drawing-room, or the Frobishers', or the Masons'. She saw nothing wrong, nothing missing, yet she viewed it with the eyes of one who had been brought up in a shabby manor and dingy lodgings, aswarm with children. Lady Amabel had different standards.

"I must see that all is well in the dining-room."

"It is. I have just now checked. You have an admirable way of encouraging the servants to give of their best."

"I ought to look—"

"Come and sit down, Ginnie. You have no need to be in a tweak. Their opinions don't matter."

"But they do." She allowed him to lead her to a chair and sat down, stiffly upright. "If everything is not perfect, they will tell the entire Beau Monde that Lord Wooburn has married beneath him. They will hold us up to scorn, Mama and the rest of us."

"I cannot imagine either George or Aunt Matilda doing anything of the sort. They are the only ones whose esteem is worth having."

"If they went from door to door denying the scandalmongers' tales, few would heed them. Thrown mud clings." She sighed. "No, you are right. It is goosish to anticipate trouble. Perhaps nothing will go wrong."

Justin seemed dismayed, but before she could ask him why, the Parringales came in. She had no further chance to speak to him before Reynolds announced dinner and George Medford offered Lady Wooburn his arm to go through to the dining-room.

As it was a house party, not a formal dinner, Ginnie had not arranged the placement at table. She found herself going in with Alfred Bascom. She looked anxiously at the table. Everything was in order; the dishes, hot and cold, looked attractive and appetizing. The footmen were neat and properly impassive. She nodded her approval to Reynolds.

Seated, she let Mr. Bascom's babble of tailors and boot-makers wash over her. Though caper-witted, he was at least not malicious. Colin, called in to make up the numbers until Lord Trenton arrived, was valiantly entertaining Aunt Matilda. Lydia appeared to be dazed by Lord Pierce's witticisms, and Gilbert had a faraway look on his face.

Justin was next to Lady Amabel, of course. However, he was not talking to her. He appeared to be trying to watch every move of Reynolds and the footmen, as if his very gaze could ensure that all went well. Ginnie wished she could reassure him that the conduct of the butler and his underlings was the least of her worries.

The fragrantly steaming soup was served and a footman removed the tureen from its place before the

earl. Another brought a pair of dishes from the sideboard to replace it. As he lifted the covers, an expression of horrified nausea spread across his face and he
staggered backwards.

Instantly the earl and Lady Trenton clapped their
napkins to their faces. A moment later the entire room
was filled with a foul smell, an indescribably revolt-
ing stink of rotting meat. Gagging, choking, retch-
ing, diners and servants alike fled the room.

Only Ginnie, Colin, and Reynolds paused in their
flight. Masked with napkins, trying not to breathe,
they stopped at the end of the table and stared down
for a moment at the reeking dish. On it lay several
toadstools, pale-stemmed, with narrow, dark brown,
slimy caps.

Reynolds dropped a cover over them. The stench
subsided a trifle.

"Stinkhorns," Colin announced.

Moving towards the door, Ginnie took a shallow
breath, just enough to speak. "The twins," she
snarled. "I'll slaughter them."

"I'll do it for you," her brother offered.

"No, I want to kill them with my own hands."

"I'm that sorry, miss," said Reynolds. "I ought
to've caught it."

"How could you guess?"

They moved on into the hall, closing the door behind them. Someone had opened the wide front door
and the diners stood on the steps, breathing deeply.
Fragments of indignant comments reached Ginnie's
ears: "Disgusting..." "Never been so affronted..."
"Utterly disgraceful..."

"Go and explain to them, Colin. Tell them it was a childish jape." She had tried so hard! Tears of despair rose as she turned to the stout butler. "Reynolds, pray serve a collation in the breakfast room as soon as you possibly can."

"Of course, miss." His kindly, worried eyes studied her. "Don't take it to heart, miss."

"I'll kill the brats!" Bent on vengeance and on hiding her humiliation, she sped to the stairs and hurried upwards.

She had reached the landing leading to the day nursery when Justin's voice halted her.

"Ginnie, wait a minute."

She kept her back to him, not wanting him to see the tears streaking her face. If he raked her over the coals, she'd have nothing left to do but throw herself in the lake.

"Ginnie, look on the bright side." Addressing her stiff back, he sounded positively cheerful.

"Bright side!" she snapped. "What bright side?"

"With any luck, they will all leave first thing in the morning."

"To spread tales about us. Oh, how could Jack and Jimmy do this to me? I cannot imagine why no one saw—or smelled—and stopped them."

"To tell the truth, I did see them."

Incredulous, she swung round. "You saw them put those toadstools in the dining-room and did nothing?"

"I didn't know exactly what they were up to, though naturally I guessed it was mischief. I didn't prevent it because I hoped—"

"You hoped to see me humiliated before your guests!" Trembling with outrage, wrath and hurt, she glared at him, blinking away tears she could not control.

"Don't be a peagoose. I—"

"Peagoose!"

"The incident hardly redounded to *my* credit, either," he pointed out in a tone of utmost reason.

"You should have thought of that sooner! I see it all. You wanted your beloved Lady Amabel to be sure she has no rival in me, to know I am beneath her notice."

"Ginnie, no."

"You are despicable."

"You don't understand..."

"I understand perfectly well. I should have trusted my first impression of you. I should never have relaxed my guard."

He stepped forward and the light from a wall sconce behind him fell on her face. "Ginnie, don't cry. I can't bear it."

"I'm not crying!" she said furiously.

Next moment she was swept into his arms. "You *don't* understand, my darling. It isn't Amabel I love, it's you."

For an instant her heart stood still. She stared up at him through a mist of tears.

He loved her?

And yet Lady Amabel had made it quite plain that she expected to marry him, and he had not denied it. He loved her, Ginnie, but he was going to wed Lady Amabel anyway. Did he suppose that she would consent to be his mistress? If only she had never allowed him to kiss her!

His lips touched hers. She wrenched herself from his embrace and slapped his face with all her might.

# CHAPTER EIGHTEEN

RUEFULLY FINGERING his stinging cheek, Justin watched Ginnie march down the stairs, her back straight and head high. What the devil was going through the little spitfire's mind now?

He had not chosen a propitious moment to declare his love, he acknowledged. He should have realized that with her emotions overwrought, she was bound to continue to misinterpret everything he said. The need to chase the misery from her eyes had overcome his discretion. All he had accomplished was to convince her of his duplicity.

At one stroke he had doubled his own difficulties. Now he had not only to persuade Amabel she did not wish to marry him, but also to induce Ginnie to believe in his love.

He had fancied that she might already love him. Her violent reaction to his attempted kiss had shaken that conceit, he reflected gloomily, following her slowly down the stairs. He had won her trust and thrown it away again. Damn the twins!

The thought of the twins reminded him of his affronted guests. Little as he wished to face them, he had a duty to act as a solicitous host.

He made his way to his chamber. By the time he reached a looking-glass, the mark of Ginnie's hand on his cheek had faded to a blurred pink patch. The application of cold water and a vigorous rubbing of his whole face with a towel concealed the evidence. Reluctantly he went downstairs.

The sound of voices drew him towards the breakfast room. Through the open door he saw people helping themselves to food from the sideboard, seated at the table eating, or carrying their plates through to the morning room.

Reynolds was the first to notice Justin's arrival. He came over, looking anxious. "Miss Webster's orders, my lord," he said.

"Excellent." Even in her distress, she had remembered to arrange for their guests' comfort. He was proud of her.

"Has miss recovered her spirits?" the butler asked hopefully, and Justin realized the man's anxiety was not for his approval of the dinner arrangements but for Ginnie's welfare.

"I doubt Miss Webster will come down this evening."

Reynolds nodded with a mournful expression and went about his duties. Justin entered the room.

Aunt Matilda, at the table, summoned him to her side with an imperious gesture. "Well, Justin, I gather a pair of rapscallions from the schoolroom were responsible for our discomfiture. A most ingenious trick. Hardwick is constantly complaining that his officers lack inventiveness and initiative. You had best buy your twins a pair of colours apiece."

Justin grinned. "They are a little young as yet, Aunt, but I shall bear your recommendation in mind."

"Little horrors," said George, sitting opposite. "Justin, do you recall when you and I—"

"Spare me! Your reminiscences will ruin my credit." Justin saw that Colin and Gilbert were eyeing him with interest. Whatever discreditable prank George had been about to reveal, the lads were not going to let him escape recounting it at a later date.

Lady Trenton, Lord Pierce, and Ferdie Parringale were sitting with stiff disapproval painted on their countenances. Justin apologized to them for the contretemps. Unfortunately, none of them announced that they would be departing on the morrow. He went through to the morning room.

Lydia jumped to her feet from her place on a sofa beside Lady Elizabeth. She hurried to him. "Is Ginnie dreadfully upset? Should I go to her, Justin?"

He hesitated. He could not guess whether Ginnie might wish for her sister's comforting presence or prefer to be alone. For his own sake, the longer she had to calm down before she disclosed his supposed iniquity, the better. "I believe she will like you to stay and support Lady Elizabeth," he suggested.

"Oh yes, I shall. Lizzie is a dear. I told her she would not be so sadly timid if she had naughty little brothers like mine."

"Very likely," he said drily. For Lydia, the insight was amazingly acute. An overprotective elder brother might well account in part for Elizabeth's shyness.

He went over to his father, though he was far from sure what to say. It was not his place to apologize to the earl for the misbehaviour of his countess's children. To his relief, Lord Wooburn's eyes were twinkling.

"Hey, my boy, those young 'uns liven the place up a bit, don't they? I've been telling Emma some of the things your uncle and I used to get up to in our salad days."

"Boys will be boys," said Lady Wooburn placidly.

Seated nearby, Lady Amabel stared at the earl and countess with incredulous disdain. Justin could avoid her no longer. He crossed to her side.

"I trust you have recovered your appetite?" he enquired, regarding the almost-empty plate she held.

"If I have, it is no thanks to those guttersnipes your father has seen fit to take into his house."

"I shall quite understand if you wish to leave in the morning, Lady Amabel."

"My father does not arrive until the day after tomorrow," she reminded him in arctic tones.

"A household containing two such enterprising youngsters cannot be congenial to you."

"I assume the boys will be whipped until they regret their wickedness, and by the time we are married they will have been dispatched to school."

So she still wanted and expected an offer! Justin was tempted to inform her then and there that she was the last female he'd ever consider making his wife. However, if it was cowardice to shrink from acting the inevitable scene before guests and family, then he was a coward.

"I must make my excuses to Lady Pierce and Mrs. Parringale," he said noncommittally, and moved on.

By the time he had smoothed their ruffled feathers, he was hungry. He returned to the breakfast room. Ginnie was there.

How could he have doubted her mettle? Self-possessed, though pale and subdued, she was offering sincere apologies to George and Aunt Matilda for her brothers' mischief, and gratefully receiving their reassurances.

The regrets she tendered to Lady Trenton, Lord Pierce, and Mr. Parringale were less sincere and considerably abbreviated, Justin noted with amusement. His words about the comparative value of their esteem had borne fruit. He longed to take her in his arms and insist that she listen to his explanations. Nonetheless, as she turned to go through into the morning room, he moved to the sideboard, out of her way, without a word. It would be best to give her wounded sensibilities time to recover, he decided.

For the rest of the endless evening, she avoided him, and he made no attempt to speak to her.

IN THE NIGHT it rained. Though the morning was grey and chilly, Justin went for his usual solitary ride, rejecting even George's company. As he circled the end of the house, he saw Jack and Jimmy sneaking out of a side door, doubtless to escape recriminations.

Sooner or later they must be disciplined, he thought as he rode on. The longer it was put off, the more difficult it would be. He accepted that neither his father nor their mother was in the least likely to lay down the law. It was his responsibility, and Ginnie's, and he could do nothing without her concurrence. Therefore he could with a good conscience stop worrying about the twins for the moment and contemplate the far-more-interesting problem of winning their sister.

As for Lady Amabel, he had no wish to mortify her, but if she refused to take any of the broad hints she had been given, he'd be forced to tell her outright that he was not going to ask for her hand.

Satisfied with this conclusion, he turned Prince Rurik's head homeward. They approached the house through the wood at the east end of the lake, as they had that fateful day when the stallion had thrown him, almost at Ginnie's feet, and he had called her a strumpet. After such a start, no wonder the road to love was beset with thorns!

As he reached the edge of the wood he saw the twins perched in the ancient, leaning willow over the fishing pool. They wielded nets on long poles that he recognized from his childhood. What was next, he asked himself wryly, minnows in the claret?

Intent on their business, they did not hear Prince Rurik's hooves on the rain-softened ground. Justin rode on. He'd tell Miss Tullycombe where the rascals were to be found.

He had ridden no more than ten paces when a splash and a scream behind him made him draw rein.

"Jimmy! Help! Oh, help, someone, please, he'll drown! Help!"

The frantic voice was followed by another splash. By that time Justin was halfway back to the pool. How deep was it? Deep enough to drown two small boys, he feared.

He tossed his hat aside and flung himself from Prince Rurik's back. One of the twins was swimming in the murky water. Of the other there was no sign.

"Jimmy slipped and hit his head. I can't find him!"

"Get out of my way."

Galvanized by the boy's terror, Justin didn't pause to remove coat or boots, but jumped in. The water reached his chin. Stirring up mud and rotting leaves, he waded towards the overhanging tree, flailing desperately with both arms.

His legs met an obstruction, heavy but shifting before him. He took a deep breath and dived. His hands met cloth, grasped, and tugged. Even as he pulled the child to the surface he turned back towards the bank.

Jack's freckles stood out starkly on his white face. "Is he dead?" he whispered.

"I don't know." Justin laid Jimmy on the mirey bank, face down, and heaved himself out of the lake. Trickles of water ran from the boy's mouth and nose. He lay limp, unmoving.

Justin seized him by the ankles and hoisted him aloft. Water gushed from him. He began to choke and splutter.

Overwhelmed with gratitude to Providence, Justin said shakily, "No, he's not dead. But I must take him home at once."

Jimmy was still insensible. Blood oozed from a gash on his temple. Justin draped him over Prince Rurik's withers, blessing his mount's patience and good manners. He set his foot in the stirrup.

"Don't leave me behind!"

He turned and swung Jack up onto the horse's rear. "Hold on to the back of the saddle." Awkwardly he mounted between the boys. "Now hold my coat. Tightly." Lifting Jimmy and cradling him in one arm, he set Prince Rurik to a gallop.

When they reached the house, he swung down with Jimmy, lent a hand to Jack to slither to the ground, and abandoned the stallion to find his own way to the stables. Squelching and dripping, he strode into the hall with Jack scuttling at his heels.

"Send for the doctor," he snapped at the stunned footman stationed there. "It's urgent." The footman ran. Justin took the stairs two at a time, shouting as he went, "Ginnie! Ginnie, where are you? Ginnie!"

She met him on the landing. "Good gracious, Justin, hush. You and I are early risers, but some people are still asleep. What . . . Jimmy!" She paled. "What happened? Bring him to my chamber."

"He slipped and hit his head and fell in the lake," Jack babbled, reaching for her hand as they hurried along the passage ahead of Justin with his burden. "I couldn't see him. I was scared till Justin came. Lots of water came out of his mouth. Will he get well?"

"I don't know, sweetheart." She cast a fearful glance backwards and then, regardless of her crisply clean lavender muslin, put her arm around her brother's filthy, soaking shoulders in a quick hug.

"I don't believe he was in the water more than a minute and a half," Justin said as she opened her chamber door. "He started breathing again on his own, but he hasn't regained consciousness. I've sent for the doctor."

He set the limp child down on a chair and Ginnie at once started to strip him. "He's so cold," she whispered. She looked round. "Jack, take off those wet clothes and wrap yourself in my dressing-gown. And you, too, Justin. I mean, go and change before you take a chill."

Appreciating her common sense even in a crisis, Justin nodded. "I'll come right back," he promised. He went out to the landing again, leaned over the balusters and roared, "Hot bricks! Warming pans! Where is everyone?"

Reynolds appeared below, his moon face raised. "At once, my lord. The doctor's sent for. How is the lad, my lord?"

"Unconscious."

The butler looked grave. "Nurse'll be down in a moment to help Miss Webster, my lord. And Mr. Tebbutt's on his way to your chamber. You'll be wanting a hot bath."

"No time." All he wanted was to be at Ginnie's side, to hold her hand and support her at the child's bedside. He turned away to go to his room and found the landing crowded with ladies and gentlemen in various stages of undress, all clamouring for an explanation.

As he impatiently told them what had happened, George kindly removed a decorative strand of waterweed from his neck. He answered a few questions, then, beginning to shiver, he said, "Excuse me, please. I must change."

Chattering, they dispersed to their chambers. Only Lady Amabel remained, an elegant figure in a robe of white silk embroidered with huge cabbage roses.

She studied him, from lank, dripping hair, past sodden, muddy clothes, to soggy boots.

"Why, Justin," she observed in a light, amused voice, "the country does not suit you, I vow."

He grinned at her.

WRAPPING JIMMY in her warmest shawls, Ginnie tucked him into her bed. She heard Justin, outside, shouting for hot bricks, and at the same time she listened to Jack's stumbling, shivering tale.

"And he couldn't swim, even though Colin taught us, 'cos he hit his head. And I didn't know what to *do*, Ginnie. And then Justin came riding like a knight in a story, 'cept he didn't have a sword and shield and armour, like they do. And I knew everything would be all right."

Justin was a hero.

"So he put me up on Prince Rurik, too, and we galloped home. He's a Trojan, Ginnie. I'm sorry we did all those things. Only, is Jimmy going to die?"

This anguished question was answered by the victim himself. He opened blue eyes, sat up, and said, "'Course I'm not, but my head hurts. And I'm hungry."

"Me, too," said Jack, at once accepting that his brother must be on the mend if his mind was already on his stomach. "We went out before breakfast."

"You *wretched* children!" Ginnie exploded with relief. "Jimmy, lie down this instant. You are not to move until the doctor comes. Jack will tell you what happened while I order you something to eat." She looked round as the door opened. "Oh, Nurse, he has come to his senses at last."

The plump, motherly woman nodded. "Imps o' mischief be hard to kill," she said tolerantly. "You heard your sister, Master Jimmy. Do as you're told and lie down. Now, Master Jack, what've you been up to?"

Lydia rushed in. "Justin says...oh, thank heaven!"

Leaving the twins in good hands, Ginnie decided to reassure Justin before she ordered their breakfast. She had been perfectly horrid to him last night, and now he had heaped coals of fire on her head by saving his tormentor's life. She went towards the landing.

As she reached the end of the passage, she saw him, still dripping, standing on the far side of the stairs with the immaculate, beautiful Lady Amabel, stylish even in *déshabillé*. Ginnie sternly extinguished a flash of wicked jealousy.

He was a hero, she reminded herself. Heroes won fair ladies and lived happily ever after. It was her misfortune that the fair lady he had chosen was not herself. All that was left to her was to pray he'd be happy with Lady Amabel.

She was about to withdraw when she overheard what he was saying.

"On the contrary, ma'am. Far from being ill-suited, I intend to make my home in the country. London would seem dull indeed compared to the exciting life I lead here. However, since the country clearly does not suit *you*, may I suggest that you return to Town forthwith?"

Lady Amabel glared at him with baffled fury, turned on her heel, and stalked away.

"Justin." At Ginnie's soft call he turned and came towards her, an odd smile on his face, holding out both hands to her. "Jimmy has recovered his senses. He is complaining of hunger! Oh, Justin, I am so sorry." She gave him her hands.

"Sorry?"

"That the twins caused a quarrel with Lady Amabel. Surely you can heal the breach. Surely they have not spoiled your chances?"

"Good Lord, no, far from it. They have rescued me from a frightful fate."

She looked up at him uncertainly. "You do not wish to marry Lady Amabel?"

"My darling hedgehog, how could I possibly be happy with someone who objects to wet, muddy clothes?"

Suddenly the most important thing in the world was to demonstrate to him that *she* had no objection to wetness or mud. She threw her arms about him, thus transferring a goodly portion of each to her own person.

He didn't seem to mind. In fact, he aided the process by clasping his arms about her. He held her tightly and kissed her with passion, with ardent tenderness, and, for the first time, without a trace of guilt.

Locked in his damp embrace, Ginnie felt no chill. A tingling heat spread through her body, and yet she shivered with desire. Justin was instantly solicitous, though his clasp did not loosen one iota.

"Lord, you'll be catching cold next. I've soaked you. Come and help me get out of these wet clothes," he suggested with a hopeful gleam in his eye, "and then I'll help you."

"I am not a strumpet," said Ginnie, indignation flaring.

"I know, my little hedgehog. I suppose you mean to make me wait until we are married."

"Yes, but by all means let us be married soon," she said dreamily, kissing the corner of his mouth. Then she pulled away a little and frowned at him. "You called me a hedgehog," she accused. "Twice."

"I *adore* hedgehogs," said Justin, and kissed her again to prove it.

# HARLEQUIN®

## REGENCY ◆ ROMANCE™

## Deck the halls . . .

You'll be dreaming of mistletoe right along with our Regency heroines this holiday season when you meet the men of *their* dreams.

Celebrate the holidays with some of your favourite authors as they regale you with heartwarming stories of Christmas past.

In November, get in the spirit with *Mistletoe and Mischief* by Patricia Wynn. In December, curl up with *Sarah's Angel* by Judith Stafford and *A Christmas Bride* by Brenda Hiatt. Then enjoy.

Harlequin Regency Romance—our gift to you.

Available wherever Harlequin books are sold.

*1993 Keepsake*

# CHRISTMAS

*Stories*

Capture the spirit and romance of Christmas with KEEPSAKE CHRISTMAS STORIES, a collection of three stories by favorite historical authors. The perfect Christmas gift!

Don't miss these heartwarming stories, available in November wherever Harlequin books are sold:

ONCE UPON A CHRISTMAS by Curtiss Ann Matlock
A FAIRYTALE SEASON by Marianne Willman
TIDINGS OF JOY by Victoria Pade

## ADD A TOUCH OF ROMANCE TO YOUR HOLIDAY SEASON WITH KEEPSAKE CHRISTMAS STORIES!

HX93

**MEN** MADE IN AMERICA

Fifty red-blooded, white-hot, true-blue hunks
from every State in the Union!

Look for MEN MADE IN AMERICA! Written by some
of our most poplar authors, these stories feature fifty of
the strongest, sexiest men, each from a different state in
the union!

Two titles available every other month at your favorite
retail outlet.

In November, look for:

STRAIGHT FROM THE HEART by Barbara Delinsky
(Connecticut)
AUTHOR'S CHOICE by Elizabeth August (Delaware)

In January, look for:

DREAM COME TRUE by Ann Major (Florida)
WAY OF THE WILLOW by Linda Shaw (Georgia)

**You won't be able to resist MEN MADE IN AMERICA!**

**Where do you find hot Texas nights, smooth Texas charm and dangerously sexy cowboys?**

*Crystal Creek*™

## GUITARS, CADILLACS
### Country music—Texas style!

Jessica Reynolds should be on top of the world. Fans love her music and she is about to embark on a tour that will make her name a household word. So why isn't her heart singing as loudly as her voice? Could it have something to do with Crystal Creek's own sheriff? Wayne Jackson is determined to protect Jessie from the advances of overzealous fans...and big-time gamblers. Jessie can't help but hope that his reason for hanging out at Zack's during her gigs is more personal than professional.

**CRYSTAL CREEK** reverberates with the exciting rhythm of Texas. Each story features the rugged individuals who live and love in the Lone Star State. And each one ends with the same invitation...

### Y'ALL COME BACK...REAL SOON

Don't miss **GUITARS, CADILLACS** by Cara West.
Available in November wherever Harlequin Books are sold.

---

If you missed #82513 *Deep in the Heart*, #83514 *Cowboys and Cabernet*, #82515 *Amarillo by Morning*, #82516 *White Lightning*, #82517 *Even the Nights are Better*, #82518 *After the Lights Go Out*, #82519 *Hearts Against the Wind* or #82520 *The Thunder Rolls*, and would like to order them, send your name, address, zip or postal code, along with a check or money order for $3.99 for each book ordered (do not send cash), plus 75¢ ($1.00 in Canada) for postage and handling, payable to Harlequin Reader Service, to:

| In the U.S. | In Canada |
|---|---|
| 3010 Walden Ave. | P. O. Box 609 |
| P. O. Box 1325 | Fort Erie, Ontario |
| Buffalo, NY 14269-1325 | L2A 5X3 |

Please specify book title(s) with your order.
Canadian residents add applicable federal and provincial taxes.

CC-9

# FLASH: ROMANCE MAKES HISTORY!

History the Harlequin way, that is. Our books invite you to experience a past you never read about in grammar school!

Travel back in time with us, and pirates will sweep you off your feet, cowboys will capture your heart, and noblemen will lead you to intrigue and romance, *always* romance—because that's what makes each Harlequin Historical title a thrilling escape for you, four times every month. Just think of the adventures you'll have!

So pick up a Harlequin Historical novel today, and relive history in your wildest dreams....